The Girl in the Coffee House

Sirjandeep Kaur Ubha

Anecdote
Publishing House
For the love of quality reading!

Anecdote
Publishing House
For the love of quality reading!

anecdotepublishinghouse.com
champreaders.com

Anecdote Publishing House
2nd Floor 2/15 Lane no. 2 Ansari Road, Daryaganj-110002
Email: info@anecdotepublishinghouse.com
Website: anecdotepublishinghouse.com

Published by Anecdote Publishing House

First Edition 2025
ISBN 978-81-988015-8-6
MRP ₹ 350

Book Promoted and Marketed by Champ Readers Pvt. Ltd.
Editorial Process: Team StoryWell
Cover design by: The Code Design Studio
Layout by: Arivazhagi Balasundaram
Printed by Thomson Press (India) Ltd, New Delhi

The Girl in the Coffee House

ABOUT THE AUTHOR

Sirjandeep Kaur Ubha hails from a family of writers in Punjab. She has completed her master's in Human Resources & Organisational Behaviour from the London School of Economics and Political Science. Having a creative flair and the creative atmosphere while growing up, Sirjan also delved into writing. She has written three books: Whispers of the Heart, a novel- The Triumph and her last novel, 'To Skies and Waters'. Sirjan was also nominated for the Sahitya Akademi Yuva Puruskar for her last novel and was shortlisted among the top 7 novels in the country.

Acknowledgment

"*Dekhi Jaegi*"

This word is etched in my mind and soul, and it defines how I operate in life. I remember starting this journey a long time ago, but somehow, I couldn't finish it the way I had wished. Still, I kept going. And I know it wouldn't have been possible to continue without the unwavering support of certain people in my life.

First and foremost, to God Almighty – whom I honestly talk to like a friend because that's my idea of religion and this superpower – thank you, Bro, whoever you are, wherever you are, in whichever form you are. Thanks for always having my back!

To my family – Dad, thank you for the constant push. I truly don't think I'd be where I am today without your support. Mom, Sohaj Veerji, Bhabhi, Papa, Vaddi Ma, Elahi – thank you for always rooting for me. Sukhan, Sukrat, Maasi, Chachu, Simmi, Vishav Veerji, Bhua, Fufar Ji, Seerat, Super – thank you for being my cheerleaders along the way.

To my husband Kunal – you are a new addition to my life but now, the rest of my life. I couldn't be more grateful for you. Thank you for continuing to encourage me and for always ensuring I get to chase my dreams. It's hard to put into words how much the support of a partner can change one's life – so thank you, truly.

To my in-laws – Mom, Dad, and the entire family – thank you for giving me the space to grow and for always showering me with your blessings.

To my friends who are like family – Mannat and Anmol – thank you for being my pillars, my sisters, my confidants, and my go-to people in both sunshine and storms. I love you both!

To the Book Cover Designers – The Code Design Studio – thank you for bringing my vision to life and creating the most perfect book cover I could have imagined.

And lastly, my heartfelt thanks to the entire team at Anecdote for bringing this work to life. It's because of you that this book will see the light of day.

CONTENTS

Hi, I am Riya. I hail from Dehradun…
There's more to me and my story. Go on…

Chapter 1

Moving to Delhi

As I opened the door of my cab, my feet landed squarely in a deep pothole. It was raining heavily and the last thing I wanted was my umbrella throwing tantrums. But here I was, in "*dil walon ki dilli*" being welcomed with tears and potholes.

"Madam, 670 Rs please," said the cab driver.

"Sure, one moment please," I said and handed him the money. I hadn't stopped crying the entire time. I had had the worst possible fight with my parents before I moved to Delhi for my research.

I picked up my stuff and contacted the broker. But to my surprise, he was already in the building waiting for me.

"Hi Madam, welcome," he said.

"Well, thank you very much," I replied, wiping away my tears and composing myself.

He seemed very happy and was kind enough to help me move my luggage to the apartment.

"Has this pothole been here for a long time?" I asked with disbelief in my own sentence.

"Madam, it will be fixed within a few weeks," he replied without really answering my question and handed the keys over to me before pressing the lift button for me.

"Thanks," I replied and put my two bags and squeezed myself in the lift. The broker decided to take the stairs. There I was, in front of apartment number 24, a beautifully decorated hallway with a European touch. The door knob seemed from the old era with (intricate carvings on it) beautiful work done on it. There were three other apartments on the same floor with similar architecture on the doors. I was excited to know who my new neighbours would be, but decided to let the introductions happen gradually.

To my surprise, the apartment was, without-a-doubt the best apartment I had lived in.

It looked better than the pictures. Right as I entered, there was a living room with the TV facing the main door and a huge pot with a beautiful green plant in it. I was a very plant person and it seemed the owner must be the same too.

I kept my bags on the side and waited for the broker to come up. There was a beautiful green sofa which looked like a sofa-cum-bed to me with a round glass table in the center. I sank into the sofa, hoping the fatigue would fade away. The broker walked in, carrying a stack of papers as I had left the door open. "Madam, can you please sign the agreement," he asked, handing the agreement over to me.

I took it and signed the agreement so the broker could leave and I finally rest.

"Madam, please let me know if you have any problems. I am just a call away," he said before leaving.

"Absolutely *bhaiya*, thanks," I replied and locked the door as he left the apartment.

I moved my luggage to a corner near the sofa and then ventured on a quick tour of the house. Right beside the living room was the kitchen, with a door. The shelves had utensils stacked in a neat manner.

The fridge had a note that said, "Welcome, hope your stay here at this apartment is comfortable, Arun."

Well, that was a sweet gesture. I've always felt something deeper with the way houses are built. Home for me is like a safe haven where you come back to – it's always there, no matter what. So, whenever I moved houses, I ensured that the place was beautifully done. With these thoughts, I passed the hallway, which led to the bedroom, well-lit with huge windows on each side of the bed behind it. There was a study table on one side and the other side of the room had an attached washroom. There was no balcony in this house but I was glad that it was well lit with huge windows. That was sufficient for me to interact with the outside world while being on my own. I went to freshen myself up and use this beautifully and architecturally done washroom. I had been the kind of person who liked to settle down, and properly unpack things the same day. So without further ado, I started unpacking my bags. The cupboards in the room had sufficient space for me not to worry about keeping everything cluttered. I played music on my speakers to vibe along while unpacking. It took me two hours to unpack, after which I decided to give my body a break and crashed. I woke up only after two hours when I heard noises from the streets. In the evenings, Hauz Khas had a different vibe and I could clearly see why now that I was here.

I was new to Delhi and it only seemed fair to venture out and explore the area a bit. Groceries needed some attention too.

"Madam, we make your way here, we have happy hours going on," "Madam, you'll get the best cocktails on the street and it's happy hours, so do not wait!!"

Hauz Khas Village has a lot of pubs, bars, clubs, and restaurants of different cuisines. Even though I wasn't in the mood for a drink, I decided moving into a new city merits one – without a doubt! I went ahead, sat at the bar which had happy hours as it seemed like a quieter place and ordered myself a glass of red wine.

"Madam, here you go...Your wine," said the bartender.

"Thank you," and I immediately paid.

He nodded with a smile. I was just soaking in the feeling of finally being in Delhi and welcoming myself with a drink.

In the coming week, my plan was to settle in completely, explore the neighbourhood thoroughly, identify my future "go-to" spots and maybe meet a friend or two. I hardly knew anyone in Delhi.

I left the bar and walked toward my apartment. As I got closer, I noticed a beautifully designed coffee shop that immediately caught my eye. Being a coffee enthusiast, I thought I had found my new spot – a perfect place to work on my research. I looked forward to visiting the shop the next morning.

Right behind my apartment, there was a grocery store. I picked up some bread, eggs, milk, pancake mix, fruits, and a few vegetables, and I was all set.

"Hi," said a voice behind me as I was waiting for my lift.

I turned and saw a lady, likely in her 60s, with a fair complexion and a graceful presence. Her wrinkled yet lovely eyes sparkled behind round glasses, and her lean build was complemented by a broad, cheerful smile.

"Hello," I replied, glancing at her and her neatly tied hair in a bun. She wore a beautiful kurta with juttis.

"Are you new to the building?" she asked.

"Oh yes. I just moved to the 4th Floor," I replied.

"Oh nice, I live in flat no. 22 on the 4th floor," she smiled, and pressed the lift button.

"Oh, how lovely! Have you been here long?" I enquired.

"Yes, I used to live with my husband. After he passed away, I have been living here on my own. My kids visit once in a while," she said.

"Oh, I'm so sorry to hear that. I can't imagine how difficult it must be," I replied.

"You get used to it. That's life, I suppose," she said with a smile, adding, "Well, take care and let me know if you need any help with anything. You should come by for tea once you're settled." She then slowly moved toward her apartment.

"Absolutely, I'll see you soon," I replied, heading toward my own apartment.

Once inside, I felt a weight on my chest. I couldn't help but ponder on the fragility of life. To spend so many years with someone only to eventually lose them – how terribly painful that must be. I put the groceries in the refrigerator and sank into the couch, lost in thoughts about life and its twists.

Chapter 2

Settling in...

A month in Delhi, I felt like it was warming up to me. The hustle and bustle of Hauz Khas, with its busy roads and weekend gatherings, showed a lively blend of corporate professionals unwinding and college students creating memories. It was fascinating to see how people at different stages of life engaged in similar activities, each in their unique way. Delhi was beginning to feel like home.

"Hi Rumi Aunty," I greeted her as I left the building for Elysian Coffee Shop. Rumi Aunty had become a comforting presence in this new town. We would chat over tea at her place, and I'd listen to her stories of old-time romance and simpler things.

"Hello, *beta,*" she responded with a smile, "Back to your research?"

"Yes, work is in full swing. I'm hoping to make progress with my literature review," I replied.

"That's amazing! Keep at it," she encouraged, before continuing on her way.

I headed towards the coffee shop. Elysian Coffee Shop had become my work space, fostering creativity and focus. The place featured wooden floors, square tables – mostly for two, with a few larger ones – and an abundance of plants. The large windows at the back opened to a backyard garden, giving a hill station vibe. Painted in cream with wooden furniture, it gave off a classy, warm ambience. By now, Tina, Harry, and Riya had become familiar and they knew my usual order: a latte with almond milk and a butter croissant.

"Hi Tina," I greeted her as I walked into the coffee shop.

Tina was a petite girl with a lean physique. Her straight shiny hair made her look even more appealing. She was a coffee brewer with a smile on her face. I didn't know if her happiness was part of the act or if she was genuine.

I went to sit at my regular table by the window, but it was occupied by two young men. I just gave them a blank look and sat on the table next to them.

"Here's your croissant," Harry, a tall and medium-built server, said with his usual smile.

"Thanks, Harry! I hope you're doing well," I said.

"All good, Riya," he replied and returned to his duties.

I started working on my literature review. The thing with PhD is that it is overwhelming, with constant back and forth, it becomes a routine.

"Haha, bro I'm telling you, she was a weird girl; she deserved a slap," one of the young men at the table next to me said.

I couldn't help but overhear and found myself drawn to their conversation, as the comment seemed out of place.

"Uh, ah, maybe yeah," the other boy replied hesitantly, avoiding eye contact. "But Sachin, that's still not right."

I was very curious to know who and what they were talking about. They seemed to be in their mid-twenties. Sachin had a lean built with a neatly groomed beard and stylishly messy hair. He wore branded clothes, dressed elegantly in a way that highlighted his well-built physique.

The other one, whose name I didn't catch yet, was around 6 feet tall, with a wheatish complexion and a casual demeanor. He had curly hair and a clean-shaven face, contrasted sharply with Sachin. Their arguments seemed to be intense.

"Karan, you don't understand the harsh realities of this world. It's better to keep your opinions to yourself if you don't know what to do with them," Sachin said to the other young man.

"What do you even mean by that?" Karan asked, puzzled.

"Nothing, let's just finish our food and head home. Mum and Dad have planned a night for our graduation," Sachin replied.

"Fine," Karan said, and they fell into silence as they finished their meals in silence. I realised I had been staring for too long, catching Karan's eye in the process.

I blinked and refocused on my laptop, typing random words that made little sense.

They both eventually left the coffee shop, clearly regulars judging by the staff's familiarity with them.

"Bye, sir. See you soon," one of the servers said.

"Bye," they replied in unison, with Sachin leading the way and Karan following swiftly behind.

For me, it is difficult not to observe people and hear conversations around me. I like to see beyond the tip of the iceberg which is why I was intrigued by the way the two men were talking. Something seemed off about how they were talking to each other, and I couldn't help but wonder if I'd get to see them again tomorrow.

Without further ado, I went back to my research. I had a meeting with my supervisor to discuss ideas for my research. I couldn't help but keep going back to Sachin and Karan's conversation.

"Anything else for you, Riya Ma'am?" asked Harry as he noticed that my coffee cup was empty.

"Ah, nothing Harry. Thank you. I am in a bit of a hurry today but thank you so much for this," I said and began to leave.

My next stop was the University, where my meeting with the supervisor would begin.

"We are doing good so far, Riya. You have a long way to go. You can meet your fellow batchmates once in a while and see if there's something better that you can learn from them, their research and, of course, make some friends," said Mr. Roy, my Supervisor.

After my session with Mr. Roy, I headed home but decided to meet Rumi Aunty first.

As I waited outside her door, I could hear her walking up to the door and slowly unlocking it from her end. She peeked and grinned at me.

"Oh Riya!! Come inside! How is your research going?" Aunty guided me to the living room sofa.

As I entered, the furniture seemed dishevelled and there was a different scent in the room. It appeared someone had visited.

"Aunty, did you have some guests over?" I enquired.

"Ah, yes! My kids came for a quick visit. They were in town for a meeting and decided to meet for lunch. They left about 15 mins ago," she said.

"Oh, your kids? How are they doing, Aunty?" I asked curiously, making myself comfortable on her couch.

She was in the kitchen, a beautifully designed open space, where I could see her preparing green tea for both of us. It seemed like we were going to have some tea-time conversations.

"Aunty, you didn't have to," I said politely, accepting the tea, as she sat next to me.

"Please no formality *bacha*, have it," she said as she pinched my cheek lovingly.

"Sure," I smiled, taking a sip. "So Aunty, why didn't you decide to live with your kids?" I asked.

Aunty sighed and said, "I know it feels like a western concept but I am at a stage in life where I just wanted to be there for myself, live alone, without caring about what the world would think of me."

I eyed her with curiosity. "What do you mean, Aunty?" I asked.

"Hmm… let me see how to break it down to you, beta. I have two kids – a daughter and a son. My daughter suffered from bipolar disorder. I spent years and years making sure she got the best care in the world. She's doing well these days. Running a business empire and is married to an amazing man who treats her the right way," she paused to take a sip of her coffee and then continued. "My son is younger than my daughter and he was a wild child! My husband and I had to ensure he understood his sister and behaved well with her. It wasn't all easy but we managed to do it. My family was beautiful, messy, chaotic but mine. I think once my husband passed away, I decided that I could refocus on my passions and live the life I wanted to," she said and smiled.

I was quiet and listening to her fondly.

Rumi Aunty looked at me. "Beta, you are a good listener," she smiled.

"Oh, that's sweet of you to say, Aunty," I said as I wiped a tear off my eye.

"Are you okay?" she asked.

"Where do your kids live now, Aunty?" I asked

"My daughter is married and lives in the US. My son is in Mumbai. He visits often," she replied.

"Oh okay. I am sure you miss them a lot," I wondered aloud.

"I do," she smiled again. "But, you see, I am busy in my world too. Come, I'll show you my paintings. Do you have some time?" she asked.

"Do you paint? Yes! I'd love to see them aunty," I got up and followed her lead.

"Come," she said as she walked from the living hall towards a room.

She turned on the light and oh boy, was I shocked!

"Wow Aunty, that's a lot of paintings," I said with my mouth and eyes wide open.

"You are like a professional painter," I said.

"Ha-ha, I am," she said as she stood there smiling, looking at her paintings.

"Here, come take a look at this one," she said, pointing towards a painting.

That painting was a portrait of a girl in her mid-twenties, smiling with a hint of mischief in the eyes.

"Is that your daughter?" I asked.

"Yes, it is. I take so much pride in her," she said and continued, "I ensured to be with her through every moment. From my work to raising her, pretty much tried to balance everything," she said. "I raised her to be brave and now look, she is doing amazing things with her life. Half the time, you cannot even tell that there was trouble," she said.

"I am sure, Aunty," I smiled.

"Anyway, enough about me," she said, switching off the lights, and stepping out of the room. I followed her to the living room. "What about you? Do you not miss your parents?" she asked.

"I don't have the best relatio-sh sh.. relationship with my parents," I said, struggling to speak.

"Oh, I am sorry. I didn't mean to dig up old wounds," she said caressing my hand.

We sat on the sofa.

"No-No that's alright," I said and continued, "My parents had different expectations of me and I guess I never really lived up to them. I never understood their viewpoint and they never bothered to understand mine," I said.

"That's a shame. You look like an amazing woman to me," she said and continued to ask, "How old are you?"

"You take a guess, Aunty," I suggested, smiling.

"27?" she asked.

"28," I said and smiled. "Life's been a roller coaster, so I needed something now to sort of keep me on my toes. PhD seemed like something I had always wanted to pursue so here we are!" I said, conveniently changing the topic.

"Well, that's great and I am happy to see that you are living your dream, you are such a pretty girl." she said.

"Yeah, thank you auunty," I said and finished my green tea which had already become quite cold by then.

"I will take your leave now, Aunty," I said.

"Oh, so soon?" she asked.

"Yes, Aunty. I will come back soon. I have to wrap up some work after which, I will take a nap. I am tired," I said.

"Okay, beta, you go ahead," she said and hugged me bye.

"Bye, Aunty," I said as I left her home and she was closing the door.

I rattled my keys to the lock and after struggling for two minutes, I got in. I was tired and angry and I just don't know why. I threw the keys on the floor in anger and lay down on the sofa. It was hot and humid. I put my arms on my eyes to shield my eyes and went off to sleep.

It was 8 pm and I realised I had taken the longest nap ever. I cooked myself some brown rice with vegetables and soy sauce, switched on the TV, and watched some news.

"*Why am I feeling so low*?" I wondered.

"*Ugh, I hate it, I hate it*!" I said and started eating my rice.

"*Maybe I need a few friends or maybe I should go on dates,*" I told myself.

Within five minutes, I ended up downloading a dating app called *Java*.

"*Ah, what the heck,*" I said and made my profile on it.

I started swiping, astonished at how things had changed for our generation and it was so unsafe to just meet someone at the bar. The app seemed like an easier option but also a lifesaver for people like me who did not like too much social interaction.

In ten minutes, I had about ten matches and wondered who I should talk to first. I spent about half an hour to forty-five minutes on this app and made a conversation with this one guy.

"*Hey you seem genuine, Ms. Researcher. I feel something serious could happen here. Can I take you out for a coffee or a drink, whatever you prefer?*" asked M. Like me, he had hidden his name on the app. Although, I wasn't looking for anything serious, coffee seemed harmless to me. So, I decided to meet him the following day.

"*Hey, Do you have a place in mind or should I suggest?*" asked M.

"*Umm. Elysian Coffee House works for you?*" I asked.

"*Cool. 5 pm then?*" he asked.

"*Done. See you,*" I said.

Chapter 3

The First Date

It was my first date and I guess I had never given clothing a deeper thought before. I chose to dress up in a pink dress with very tiny flowers on it. It was a soft cotton long dress with a slit on the left side. I let my hair loose. I carried a small sling bag to go with it. I did not know what to expect of it.

I walked to my all-time favourite coffee shop. M was waiting in all black which complemented his fair complexion. He seemed 5'10 with trimmed hair with little curls that made him look cute. If elegance were a person, M would top the list, smartly dressed in baggy pants and a black shirt. He chose to wear sandals, making him appear cool and casual.

"Hey," I said as he was busy peeping into his phone.

"Oh, hi," he greeted me with a side hug.

"How are you? Please sit," he smiled and gestured to me to sit.

I sat and made a point to wave at Harry and Tina. They seemed pretty amused to see me on a date. I usually came alone and 5:30 pm was not even my usual time. I would normally be at the coffee house by 11 - 11:30 am. So naturally, there was something new for them to see.

"What would you like to have?" asked M.

"Ah, they know," I said, smiling.

"Oh? Are you a regular here?" he asked.

"Yes, I am," I said and continued, "Why else do you think I called you here?" I smiled.

"Hah interesting, I must say," he said, making a wider smile. He glanced at the menu and ordered for himself.

"So S, may I please have the pleasure of knowing your full name?" he asked

"Riya," I said.

"You look pretty, Riya. I like your brown eyes," he said and continued, "Don't you want to know my name?" he asked, even though I was going to ask this next.

"Yes, I'd appreciate that," I said, sarcastically.

"Manav," he said.

"Well, hello, Manav. It's nice to meet you," I said, looking here and there but towards him. I kept looking down, almost as if I was checking out my own footwear!

"Nice to meet you too, Riya. Feeling shy?" he asked.

"It's nothing like that," I said, nodding in mild disbelief. Did he just pass a snide comment in the first 10 minutes?

Meanwhile, my latte arrived at my table and Tina just couldn't stop smiling.

"Thanks, Tina," I said awkwardly.

"So Riya, what are you researching about?" asked Manav.

"Something in Organisational Behaviour," I replied.

"Oh, interesting. I work as a freelancer in the cybercrime space and I'm also a digital marketeer," he replied.

"Cybercrime sounds quite interesting," I said amused by his answer.

"Well, it indeed is. I get to do sneaky things," he said laughing.

"Hmm," I said, not amused.

"Are you okay?" he asked, seeing my hand curled into a fist.

"Yeah, I should tell you, this is my first date," I replied feeling all nervous.

"Oh, really! I mean that explains the nervousness. Listen, be easy. There's no judgement, here," he said.

"Well thanks," I said.

"So tell me more. Where are you originally from? How long have you been in Delhi?" he asked.

"It's been close to two months now. I am from Dehradun," I said.

"Oh wow, Dehradun! That's a beautiful place. I have been there many times, especially when my friends and I travel to Rishikesh," he said

"Well, isn't that nice," I said, almost chugging my coffee.

"Slow down, are you in a rush?" he asked, sipping his Iced Americano.

"Actually, I am. I completely forgot I had an online meeting with the supervisor and there's a lot that needs to be done with my research," I said, trying to excuse myself.

"Well okay, that was a short date. I am sorry if I offended you in any way," he said.

"No, that's not the case. Also, this one is on me." I said and left the table to go to the checkout counter.

"Hey Tina, can you please give me the cheque?" I asked Tina.

"Sure, all good?" she asked.

"Yeah, all good," I said, trying to catch my breath. I took the bill, paid, and left.

I couldn't understand my nervousness. I rushed back home as fast as I could.

"*What happened to me there?*" I questioned myself.

It looked like I got very nervous with the entire going on a date. I found it hard to interact with new people and I had to blame my parents for this. They mostly kept me away from people. My schooling wasn't the best compared to the stories

I have heard from my peers. It was only my willingness to excel that kept me afloat. This in addition to Mrs. Mira, who really helped me with my studies and sometimes, life. I felt truly alone when she left Dehradun and moved to Indore shortly after her marriage.

She used to say, "You can pursue what you desire if you have the will. If the world doesn't offer it to you, you take it for yourself," and that was what resonated with me for the rest of my life. I knew I had it in me to move forward in life and learn. I paved my way through life and moved to Delhi. My parents were never really supportive of my decisions yet I did what I had to do. I guess that is the reason why when anybody talked to me about my parents, I never really said much. I blame them for how I turned out.

I decided to start with household chores to keep my mind occupied. I started with laundry, which did the trick. It helped me calm down and get things into perspective.

An hour into the chores, I heard a knock at my door. I went and opened and it was my food delivery guy.

I was too tired to cook a meal so I had ordered some food for myself. I sat down with a news channel and finished the meal in peace. I went back to my PhD work after dinner and worked on the pointers that Dr. Roy gave to me.

As I was about to go back to sleep, a notification popped up from *Java*.

"*Hey, you okay?"* said Manav.

"*It was nice meeting you,"* it further said.

I chose not to reply to the message and turned off my mobile phone's wifi, switched off the lights, and went to sleep. It felt like my body needed rest and sleep.

I woke up feeling fresh and when I turned on my phone, there were about 5 messages

"*Look I don't know what happened but there's something in you that kind of made me want to text you… you seem like a very deep person. I like your personality and I felt drawn to you,"* said M.

"*Can we meet again? I get that you are an introvert and it was on your first date. So, let's meet at your favourite place and give it another shot?"* said M.

"*Okay Manav, Let's meet at 11:30 am today, same place?"* I asked.

"*Works,"* said M.

Today I chose not to dress up or do anything different to impress Manav. I went in my regular rugged jeans and top with sneakers. It made me feel comfortable and calm. I took my laptop because I knew I had a ton of work to do for my research, so I planned to sit there for my date.

"Hey," said Manav, putting his hand on my shoulder as I sat with my back towards the main door.

"Hey, Hi! How are you?" I said, startled.

"I am good and you?" said Manav, making himself comfortable on the chair.

"So," I started saying without really knowing what I wanted to say.

"Look, we can take this really slow. I don't think I have ever met someone who has driven me this crazy ever," he said.

"Wow, aren't you fast?" I said, smiling.

"Hah," he said, partially laughing.

"So Riya, How is your research going?" he asked when I noticed the boys, Sachin and Karan, from earlier walk in.

"Hey," he said, trying to get my attention, waving his hand in front of my face.

"Sorry," I said, "My research is going well. There's a lot to do. I'm sure you'd know a PhD is no easy task. There's a lot that goes into it," I said.

"Yeah, of course." he said and continued, "although I have never really been too studious in my life. I am more of a creative person. I like the thrill in my life. I like finding solutions to things and events," he said.

"Yeah? That sounds interesting. Are you like a detective or a criminal?" I asked.

"Haha, guess you'll never know," he said and smirked. I smiled back.

"I have ordered my coffee. What will you have?" I asked and we carried on our conversations there. But

I was more curious about Karan and Sachin. Those boys had my interest because the conversation from the other day was left behind.

They sat at the table next to me.

"Hey, where are you lost?" asked Manav.

"I am so sorry, I lose focus sometimes. Anyway, tell me about yourself. How are you single? Never dated or did breakup bring you to Java?" I asked.

"Haha, I had a girlfriend about 2 years ago. We dated for 4 years but then things didn't work out. She wanted something else from life and I was on my own journey," he replied.

"Interesting, how easy it has become to just move on these days," I said, lost in my thoughts.

"That's not the case. We tried everything to make it work but eventually decided to part ways amicably. I hold her in high regard and I am at a good place in life. In fact, she's getting married soon and I'm happy for her," he said.

"Wow, that's big. It might take a lot of courage for you to say that you are happy for her," I said.

"Not really. I mean, of course, you have your moments but it's not sad now," he replied and continued, "so anyway, here I am, ready to get into the dating world and see if something could happen."

"That's nice to hear, Manav. I have never dated in my life. I always lived in my own little world with my dreams and ambitions. So here I am, doing my own thing and experimenting with this dating world for the first time and..." I stopped mid-way and found Manav staring deep into my eyes, his eyes wide and his chin resting on his hand, so that I got slightly conscious of him being that focused.

"Ehmm, so yeah, that's about it," I finished. I realised Karan was overhearing my conversation. I smiled at him and he smiled back.

"Ah, so I am the lucky one," chirped Manav.

"Please!" I said.

"That's rude," he said, feeling a little dejected.

"No-No, I am sorry, that's my bad," I replied.

We continued our conversations and suddenly Manav's phone rang.

"Hey, sorry I need to take this," he said and got up.

"Yes, sure," I replied although he had already walked towards the other side of the coffee shop. He was gesturing a lot with his hands and it seemed like he had an important call.

Walking towards our table, he said, "I am so sorry but I have to cut short this time. There's some work emergency," he said and before I could say anything, he continued, "Can I have your number?"

"Oh, sure. Don't worry, I'll message you on Java. You go ahead and attend to your work thing," I replied, fiddling with my phone.

He smiled and left.

It felt like a relief that he had left. I guess I had a lot more warming up to do before I could be comfortable with him. But without wasting time, I opened my bag and took out the laptop to start working.

"Hey Tina," I waved at Tina because I needed another strong cup of coffee to go through the day. Tina nodded and acknowledged even before I could say anything.

"Karan, I sometimes don't understand what you do to get so much attention from Mom and Dad but anyway you are my brother so I can totally give it to you for being so weird," and he continued, "Harry, can you get us our Americanos please."

The proximity of the tables was so close that it was difficult not to pay attention to the conversations around.

"Bhaiya, I understand your frustration but it is what it is," said Sachin. It seemed from their conversation that their parents definitely loved one more than the other.

I was a single child so I didn't really know much about the difference in behaviour of parents towards their two or more children.

"How many times have you failed graduating? You are finally graduating with me," said Karan, seemingly taking a dig at Sachin.

"At least, I tried," he said, looking down and not making eye contact with Karan. I was looking towards them from the corner of my eye. I wanted to know more and more about their lives.

I was so lost in their thoughts that I didn't realise Tina was standing there with coffee in her hands.

"All good, Riya ma'am?" she asked.

"Oh yes, all good. Thank you for the coffee," I said and continued whispering, "tell me something, how long have these guys been coming here for?"

She looked towards them and said, "Oh, longer than you," and smiled. Their parents are the famous Saxenas. They own a house here but they stay in Mumbai. The kids go to college here. Parents come here quite often and they are quite well-known in this area.

"Oh, Saxenas?" I asked.

"Yes, have you heard of them?" she enquired.

"No, not really, I have heard someone talking about them at the grocery store once," I said, recalling the vague memory of that name before. She nodded in affirmation and then left.

I got down to my coffee and realised that Karan was looking at me. I was wondering if he had heard my whispers. I smiled back, waved, and got back to my research.

Chapter 4

Progress...

As I progressed in my life in Delhi, slowly, I got comfortable with the pace of life and the people around me. One fine Sunday, I was sitting at my regular spot in my regular coffee shop and there came my two curious boys.

"Oh hey, long time!" I said, looking at Karan. He looked towards me in a little bit of astonishment. We hadn't really spoken much before. We had only reached the stage of His and Hellos.

"Oh yeah, our parents were here, so we were busy there," he replied. Sachin nodded in affirmation to Karan's answer.

"Oh okay," I said and got back to my laptop without wanting to sound like a complete idiot.

"How are you," asked Karan.

"Good, thanks," I said and returned to my work. I knew I was showing more interest in their lives than they were.

I went back to my usual routine of working and they began chit-chatting. It felt like it was their safe haven too.

"I am lowkey jealous of how much Mom and Dad do for you," said Sachin.

"I'm sor..," Karan was interrupted by Sachin saying, "Are you mad? I am just joking," he said.

I was wondering *why a brother would think so* even though jealousy in kids was pretty common.

"It's not my fault, you know, that I am autistic," said Karan.

At that moment I don't know what happened but I looked towards them and uttered very loudly, "WHAT?"

They got a little creeped out and both started looking towards me.

"I am sorry, I am so sorry," I said and continued, "I don't know what just happened. I was in my own mind." I did not want to look like a stupid person who shouted out of nowhere, very evidently listening to their conversation.

They ignored my comment and carried on with their conversation.

"I am sorry Karan. I really didn't mean it this way," said Sachin.

"No, I know. It's just that sometimes I feel it is unfair to you that I get a lot of attention," he said.

"It gets to me sometimes. I just want to tell you that I am proud of you for everything you have accomplished in your life. Mom and Dad have been incredible with everything as well," said Sachin.

"I know, I cannot thank them enough," he said, getting teary-eyed.

I was a little jealous of how everyone had a good relationship with their parents.

I moved my chair a bit to hear more of what they were saying but I think my sudden movement drew the attention of the boys.

"Are you okay, miss?" asked Sachin in a very direct and heavy tone.

"Yeah, I guess I overheard you guys and I was curious," I said and smiled.

"Umm, okay," they said in unison.

Karan made a very casual face and it felt as if he wanted to say "*How weird is she*?"

I would have wondered the same. I wasn't a social person and couldn't carry myself properly in a social setup.

"Hi Tina, can you please get me a croissant," I waved at Tina so I could change the conversation and get back to my work. I guess seeing everyone has a good relationship with their parents and the thought brought back several memories.

I ate my croissant and tried not to listen to much of their conversation.

"*Hey, Meet up tonight?*" my phone buzzed with Manav's notification.

"*Hey, Sure, whatever,*" I said very impulsively without giving it much thought.

"*Umm whatever?*" said the next text.

"*9pm, dinner at my place?*" I replied.

"*See you. Text me the location,*" it said.

"*Ok,*" I replied and went to the cash counter to pay the bill, halfway looking into my phone.

"Thanks bye," I replied and left the coffee shop. I could see both Karan and Sachin looking at me. I tried to ignore them, which eventually led to me banging the door aggressively.

As I was waiting for the lift in my building, I saw Rumi Aunty stand beside me.

"Oh, hi aunty, how have you been," I asked.

"Good, you tell me? You look a little flushed, is everything okay?" she enquired, searching my face for any hints.

"Yes, just in a bad mood, but thanks for checking in," I replied without making eye contact.

Aunty seemed to be taken aback by my behaviour.

"Okay, come home if you need anything. There's nothing a cup of hot tea cannot fix," she said smiling.

I smiled, without meaning it. We both went up to our floor in silence after that. I didn't care to say bye and just went into my apartment.

It wasn't even a fraction of a second that my eyes started bawling out and within seconds I was crying and just blabbering things.

I picked up my groceries, took out a packet and started peeling off the pistachio's shell and kept doing it until I calmed down a bit.

"What do I do with these," I wondered looking at all the pistachios and started eating them one at a time. I packed the rest into a Tupperware box and kept it in the storage. I drew myself a bath, soaked my day in the water, and finally after an hour of absolutely not talking and just doing nothing, I realised it was 8 pm and I had asked Manav to come around 9.

I changed into comfortable pyjamas and turned on the news while waiting for Manav. I wasn't sure what made me call him home but it seemed like a better option than going out, considering the day I had. Manav and I had been seeing each other for a month now and this was the first time I called him home.

There was a soft knock at my door.

"Hey, come on in," I said.

"Hey," he hugged me and kissed me on my cheek.

"The house smells wonderful," he exclaimed.

"Does it? I just had a long bath, perhaps it's that," I said, shirking that conversation a little.

"Somebody had a bad day?" he said.

"No, just research," I said and continued, "Come have a seat," I gestured to him to sit on the sofa while I seated myself on the chair.

"So what do you want to do? Should we order something?" he asked.

"Ya, do you want to go for a pizza?" I asked without really making eye contact.

"Sure, that sounds good," he said.

I went on the app and ordered a pizza for the both of us.

"Are you okay, Riya? You haven't been too responsive lately. I want to know where we stand with us," he asked.

"It's nothing like that Manav, you know how introverted I am and it's a huge deal for me to be talking to you for a month now," I said and continued with a sigh in my voice, "I just don't have the best relationship with my parents and I know I haven't talked about it earlier but sometimes it just gets to me."

"Oh. I am sorry, Riya. Everything is on your own terms, right?" he said. I smiled and nodded.

"How about you? How is your relationship with your parents?" I asked. I decided to get up and sit next to him.

"It's good to be honest. My dad and I are close to each other. He's a public servant so he has less time," he said and continued, "but it's good; we like each other's company."

"That's nice. What exactly is being a public servant?" I asked.

"Similar department as mine," he said.

"Oh, okay," I said without really being satisfied with his answer.

"How's your thesis coming along?" he asked.

"Oh, it's fine. So far so good. I have a meeting scheduled with my professor tomorrow at the University," I replied.

"Okay," he said. We sat in silence for a bit. But in my heart, I knew that we were carrying on this meet-up for no reason. I had always been super protective of my energies and it felt no different this time. However, I wanted to give it a proper shot before I threw the entire thing.

There was a knock at the door and I sprang into action to open the door. My impulse reaction took Manav by surprise.

"Here we go," I said, with a smile on my face.

"Thanks, come let's eat," he said, patting his hand on the sofa, gesturing to me to sit next to him.

I smiled, raising my eyebrows, and sat next to him.

"Dig in!" he said, excitedly.

"Yes," I exclaimed and took the first slice of Pizza.

"So, you are one interesting person Riya!" he said.

"Am I?" I smiled.

"Of course, I mean obviously there seems to be some mystery but I guess I understand the discomfort of opening up to people and trying to befriend them when all your life you've not hung out much with everyone," he said.

"Yea, I was this skinny kid in school, with two braids all the time, absolutely no fashion sense but always with a keen interest in studies. You know I loved Mathematics, even though I had a hard time understanding maths, something in it excited me," I smiled.

"Yeah?" he said, curiously listening to my story.

"Yeah, but there was this teacher, Mrs. Mira, who always attended to me, took a special interest in me, and helped me learn most things. She kind of became my safe place in my school," I said, taking a bite of the pizza and continued, " I didn't change school my entire life. So, even though people knew who I was, I wasn't approached often. I wasn't bullied due to the strict rules, but I also didn't experience much love or admiration," I said, finishing my slice. "But, I know if you can't get something, you have to go after it and claim it from the world!"

"I am so sorry Riya. It's heartbreaking to hear about your troubled childhood," he said.

"Yeah, well. I did make one friend back in Dehradun – Shivani. She understood me and offered me a significant stake in her cafe. It's quite well-known, so it helped me earn a lot," I said, smiling.

"Shivani, huh?" he asked.

"Yeah, she's great. We're not really in touch, but whenever I'm back in Dehradun, I make a point to catch up with her," I said, noticing he hadn't been eating.

"Come on, eat," I urged.

"Oh, right," he said and picked up another slice which was melting with all the cheese inside it.

"I am sorry, Riya. But look at you now, doing amazing things, meeting people like me," he said, with a teasing smile.

"Of course, but the world isn't always fair, Manav. People and circumstances can be unjust to those who have done nothing wrong. We have to take charge of our own happiness, or else the world will break us apart and keep moving," I said, with a hint of frustration.

"I understand, it's definitely tough," he said, gently holding my hand.

I let him.

"You are amazing, Riya! I mean, look at you!" he marvelled.

I looked at him and smiled.

"May I?" he said, leaning closer.

I took a deep breath, and we shared a passionate kiss. It was my first kiss, so I was a bit unsure if I was doing right.

"Don't worry, I got you," he said.

"Thanks," I said, feeling a bit different after the kiss. I pulled back slightly, feeling a little distracted.

"Hey, relax. I am sorry," he said

"No, don't be. It was nice," I replied, then asked, "By the way, I usually go to Elysian Coffee House, but what other quiet places are around?"

"There are a few. I could show you sometime?" he offered.

"Yeah, sure," I said, smiling.

With that, our pizza and conversation came to an end. It felt like we had shared more this time than ever before.

"Okay, I'll head out now," he said.

"Yeah, okay," I replied, standing up. I placed the pizza box near the garbage can in the kitchen, washed my hands, and went to say goodbye.

He leaned in for a peck on my lips, and I kissed him back.

"Bye," he whispered in my ear.

"Bye," I said, locking the door after he left.

I took a deep breath, shook my head, and sank on the sofa.

That was something, I thought to myself before heading to bed.

Chapter 5
What just happened?

The next morning, waking up felt difficult. I freshened up, cooked myself some eggs, and went downstairs to eat. I needed to send a few pages of analysis to my supervisor today and meet him at the university in the evening.

As I stepped out to head to the Coffee House, I bumped into Rumi Aunty.

"Hi Aunty," I greeted her.

"Hi Beta, how are you?" she asked.

"I am fine, Aunty. How about you? I am sorry I couldn't come by yesterday; I was busy," I replied.

"I figured," she said, picking up a bag and locking her door. We walked towards the elevator together.

"Coffee House?" she inquired.

"Yeah, you know where my place is," I said with a smile.

"Of course," she said, returning the smile.

"Are you okay, Aunty? You seem a bit low," I asked.

"I'm fine, just missing my daughter today. She was unwell yesterday and had a fit because of her being a Bi-polar," she explained.

"Oh, I am sorry to hear that," I said, avoiding eye contact. "You must love her a lot."

"Of course, I do. I wish I could be there with her in the US to help, but her husband's amazing, so I feel a little more at ease," she said.

"Hmm," I responded as we exited the lift.

"I'll see you soon, Aunty," I said before heading to the coffee house.

Upon entering, I smiled at Tina and everyone and took my usual seat. Karan and Sachin were already there, looking content and animated in their conversation.

I called for Tina, who was busy arguing with a customer. Something must have happened because a person like Tina would not get upset that easy.

I opened my laptop to get some work done before my meeting with my professor, but my curiosity got the better of me. I couldn't help but eavesdrop on Karan and Sachin's conversation.

"I am so happy to hear that you're going with Mom and Dad for the vacation," Sachin said.

"I know, brother. I wish you could come too," Karan replied.

"Well, I have a lot of work to catch up on, but I'm glad you'll have fun on my behalf. Don't forget to get me those I mentioned," Sachin said.

"Of course, I will," Karan assured him.

"I'll go the next time my schedule allows," Sachin replied, the corner of my eye catching a hint of irritation. What are they talking about? Where is he going for this trip? I wondered.

"Absolutely, just don't hate me for this," Karan said.

"Me and hate you? Of course not. Look, I know I tease you about getting attention because of your autism, but I don't mean it. We can't choose what we're are born with. So I am sorry," he replied.

"Yeah," Karan responded, then continued, "Anyway, next time we'll cover Europe together. I'm happy that Mom and Dad wanted to take me on this vacation for graduating. And I want to thank you for supporting me in times of need."

"Of course, bro," Sachin replied, placing his hand on Karan's shoulder in a gesture of affirmation.

I sipped my coffee, listening patiently. It seemed that deep down, Sachin felt a bit neglected. Maybe their parents unknowingly did more for Karan, and Sachin probably didn't get everything he felt he should have.

"Tina, hi," I called out, waving Tina over to my table.

"Hi, how can I help?" she asked, her usual smile in place.

"Can I please get a croissant and one to go? Also, I'd like to buy that glass – it looks really nice," I asked.

"Yes, absolutely. I'll get that for you," she said before heading off.

I continued listening to their conversation, though I felt I was now invading their privacy.

"I need to have everything ready in 10 days," Karan said.

"It's fine, I'll help you. There's still time," Sachin replied.

"Yeah," Karan agreed.

How unfair of the parents to take one son, I thought to myself. I turned my attention back to my work.

Later, I had to meet my professor in the evening and decided it would be ideal to see Manav at a place other than the coffee shop. University might be a good choice – I decided to hang out briefly before my meeting with my supervisor.

While working, I saw Karan and Sachin preparing to leave.

"Listen, you go ahead. I'll catch up with you. I need to hand over the documents to Aarav," Sachin said to Karan.

"Oh yes, I forgot about them. I'll walk back home," Karan replied.

"Will you be okay?" Sachin asked.

"Yeah, all good," said Karan.

"Alright, I'll see you real quick," said Sachin and went on to pay the bill. After both of them left, I wrapped up my things and went to pay mine as well.

"The coffee was exceptionally good today, Tina," I told Tina with a smile.

"Thanks," she replied.

"You seem a bit off lately. Are you okay?" she said.

"No, it's just work," I replied. With everything going on – PhD, living alone, and balancing responsibilities – it wasn't that easy. I paid and left for the University.

I wandered around and then went to the campus to meet Manav. I sat on a green bench that blended into the lush greenery of the university's garden. When it was almost time for my meeting, I felt a tap on my shoulder.

"Hi," I heard a voice and turned around.

"Oh, hi, Manav," I replied.

"You look flushed," he said.

"No, I am fine," I replied.

"Oh, okay, if you say so," he said.

"Come, have a seat," I said, and kissed him on the lips as soon as he sat next to me.

"Wow, that was unexpected," he said.

"Well," I replied, looking at the trees.

"Okay," said Manav, glancing at me from the corner of his eye. "What time is your meeting?"

Ah, Yeah. What meeting? Yeah I mean I don't know what you're asking.

"Riya?" he said, tapping on my thigh.

"Yea?" I asked.

"I asked what time your meeting is," he said with a hint of hesitation.

"Oh, it's in about 15 mins," I said "Should we go get coffee from the canteen?"

"Coffee is never a bad idea," he replied.

"Okay, let's go," I said, and we both stood up to get some coffee. The park had a coffee shop at one end, just a minute's walk away.

"How was your day?" he asked, holding my hand.

I looked at him and responded, "My day was fine. I had to work a lot before coming to university."

"Oh, you could have asked me to meet you at the coffee shop rather than waiting around here," he said.

"Did I ask your opinion?" I questioned.

"Relax, Riya! What did I say to offend you?" he asked.

"No, nothing. I am sorry. I just thought you'd appreciate that I waited for you here," I replied.

"No, absolutely. It makes me feel special that you waited for me," he replied.

"Okay then, it is settled," I said with a half-smile.

Manav seemed calm and genuinely interested, evident from the efforts he was making.

"It indeed is. So, how often do you have to meet your supervisor?" he asked.

"Not that often, but I try to meet him twice a month. Otherwise, once a month works too. He felt it would be beneficial for me to stay here, meet him and the other students regularly," I replied.

"Okay, that's nice I suppose. It should help you get better results from your research because of the exposure you'll get," Manav said. Before he could say anything else, I said, "Yeah, exactly. Exposure and a few classes that I'll have to start attending soon."

"Great. That way, you'll make friends here," he replied with evident concern and enthusiasm.

"Yeah, I suppose," I said. "I have never really lived alone before. This is the first time, and it's liberating, to say the least. I know I've mentioned this before, but it reminds me of how far I've come. There's no turning back now. I have to make it in life here, and I know I will. Soon I'll start the research assistant job, and things will get better."

"I'm sure they will, Riya. Things are already great, and they'll get better. You are an ambitious person. I hope you find what you're looking for in Delhi," he said.

"Yeah," I replied, as he squeezed my hand. "Ouch."

"I am sorry, what happened?" he asked

"Nothing, it just hurt a little," I said, pulling my hand away.

"Sorry, did something happen?" he asked.

"No nothing, just a paper cut," I replied.

"Okay," he said.

We had reached the coffee house and he was much more excited than anyone else about the coffee. His energy was quite contagious.

"One Americano and one Latte, please," he asked the server.

"Sure sir," the server replied.

"You remember my order now," I asked

"Yes, of course. They don't sell croissants here, I assume?" he asked.

"No, they don't," I said, smiling. "Coffee is fine for now. I got a croissant packed from Elysian."

"Smart girl," he said.

"I know," I replied.

He paid for the coffee, and we walked towards the seating area. There weren't many students around. Some undergraduates were sitting at a table, playing poker with candies.

I looked towards them and smiled.

"You know, I never really had a great time in college. I had a friend though, Shivani who – " I started, but Manav interrupted, " …who helped you with her café, right?"

"Oh, you remember?" I asked.

"Yes, pretty much everything you say. I have a sharp memory," he replied.

"Okay. Well, I forgot I mentioned her, but yes, Shivani and I had a good time in college. She's a kind girl. Sometimes, I felt she was friends with me out of kindness because otherwise, she had a huge group of friends. Nonetheless, I'm grateful for everything she's done for me," I said.

"Well, she sounds like a nice person," he replied. "Enough about the past. Look at you doing amazing things now."

"Yea, amazing!" I emphasized.

I checked my phone and saw it was almost time to meet my supervisor.

"Are you done with your coffee," I asked politely, as I had finished mine.

"Yeah, let's just sit for two more minutes?" he suggested.

"Of course," I replied, and we sat in silence for the remaining time. I kept thinking about how my life went around and brought me where I am today. How things in life panned to make me reach here. While I was in my thoughts, I took his cup of coffee and sipped the last bit, because there's no such thing as too much coffee. He smiled.

"Should I get you another one?" he asked

"No, that's not needed. The last sip worked out well," I replied

He smiled again.

"Okay then, I better get going," I said, standing up.

"Okay, miss," he replied, also getting up. We shared a side hug and said goodbye.

"I'll see you soon," he said.

"Sure thing," I replied, walking towards the building where I had to meet my supervisor. I looked back and saw him walking in his beautiful green shirt and beige pants. He looked quite charming.

"*What a sweet boy*," I thought to myself as I entered the building.

I knocked on Mr. Roy's room, which was open, and saw him working on his laptop.

"Come on in, Riya," he said seemingly expecting me.

"Sir," I said, entering the office.

"How have you been Riya? Come, take a seat," he said, gesturing me to sit down.

"I am fine, sir," I replied.

"I was going through your work, Riya. There are several inconsistencies," he said. "It seems you are not focussed."

"No sir, I am completely focussed," I replied.

"I am telling you this because you should listen. The literature review has inconsistencies and needs better research work to begin with," he said.

"Okay sir," I said, "I'll look into and try to improve it as soon as possible."

"If you have any problem, let me know. I am also emailing you my notes for the review. See if you can incorporate the suggestions," he replied.

"Okay sir," I said.

I felt disheartened; it is the best feeling in the world.

"Don't be discouraged. Just go through my notes and see what makes sense to you. It's not that difficult if you put your mind to it. Choose better resources," he said.

"Yes sir, I'll take it into consideration," I replied.

He then explained other areas in my work that required improvement. I listened patiently, but I struggled to comprehend what he was saying.

"Okay sir, thank you for the suggestions. I'll come back in a few days with all my changes in place," I replied.

Once I was outside the campus, I rushed into an auto since my head was pounding and I desperately needed to take medicine. Exhausted and unable to relax, I took a headache pill and went straight to bed. I woke up two hours later at 7:30 pm, as I felt the need to talk to Manav. This was something new to me.

"*Hey, what are you up to?*" I texted.

"*Hey nothing, just working on something. How was your meeting?*" he replied.

"*It was fine. Can you come over?*" I asked.

"*Yeah, I can. Is everything okay?*" he asked.

"*Yeah, just felt like being with someone right now,*" I replied.

"*I'll be there as soon as I can babe,*" he texted.

Babe – This was the first time someone was calling me that. It felt weird.

"*See you,*" I texted back.

I guess right now, I just really wanted to be with someone. Manav was bringing out a side to me which

I never really explored before. I never thought I could feel loved. My gut just wanted Manav around and surprisingly that was the only thing that could have brought me peace. I have not had friends in the past and anyway being family too away emotionally, I did not feel the need to have someone with me. But I guess I was wrong. I yearned for Manav. I was feeling lonely and tired. I tidied up the living room and then settled on the sofa, waiting for Manav. When the doorbell rang, I got up to answer it, expecting to see him. I opened the door with a big smile, only to find Rumi Aunty standing there.

"Oh, Hi Aunty! How are you?" I asked.

"I am good. I just got you some home-cooked Thai food," she said.

"Oh! How sweet of you Aunty! Please come on in," I said and took the bowl with shaking hands. I was tired and my body sort of was just wanting some rest and I felt a tinge of weakness!

"Are you okay?" she questioned.

"Yes, I am, alright," I answered, coughing a bit, and sounding abrupt.

"Should I get you some water?" I asked.

"No *beta*, that's all right, I will take your leave. I have a lot to work on," she said.

"Oh okay," I replied.

She patted my shoulder and left. I went behind and before closing the door, I said, "Please take care, Aunty."

She looked back and smiled at me. *What a good kind lady*, I thought to myself. I went inside only to run back to the door to open it again. It was Manav.

"Oh, that was quick?" I said.

"Should I go back and come back a bit later?" he said, smiling.

"Sure, let's do that," I said, rolling my eyes.

He came in and we hugged each other tightly.

"How is your hand?" he asked, seeing the bruise on my hand.

"Yeah, it's all right," I replied, looking away.

"You seemed distressed in your message. Is everything okay, Riya?" he asked.

"Aren't you reading between the lines a bit too much, Manav?" I guided him to settle down on the couch with me.

"No, I don't think so. It just looked like something was bothering you," he said.

"Yeah, umm," I started to tear up, unable to finish the sentence.

"Hey, c'mon! Come here," he said and pulled me into his arms. His hand gently caressed my hair, offering comfort and sympathy.

"I... I had a troubled childhood. I wish I had understanding parents, you know. I wish they understood me as much as other parents understand their kids. Look at you, you have an amazing relationship with your father.

You can call him anytime you want. You can discuss things with him. He seems to care for you, considering how involved he keeps you in things. I always wonder what it would be like to have such a relationship, you know," I said and continued, "but I am so glad to have met you – it feels good to finally share my feelings with you."

"Oh babe, I am so glad to have met you too," he said and tightly hugged me. He continued, "I understand that your relationship with your parents is not good but it's okay, you are an adult and now you get to live however you wish to live."

"I don't think you understand," I whispered and turned away from him.

"Hey! I am sorry. I didn't mean to undervalue your feelings," he said and continued, "Come here," and he pulled me closer to him. "I am very sorry you've had to go through this in your childhood. It breaks my heart to see that you are carrying all this till now and rightfully so. But do not worry, you have me now! You have got me and please know that I have your back." He held my chin and brought it close to his face. When our eyes met, he slowly leaned in to kiss. His fingers dug into my hair, pulling me closer still. My hands travelled his neck to hold his back firmly. He paused, before holding my gaze and kissing me again. I laid back on the sofa and he was on top of me as we continued kissing. He slid his hand towards the cape of my neck and caressed me there slowly. His lips moved downwards, evoking emotions that were new to me. I closed my eyes and felt every moment of it.

"May I?" he asked, as his hands moved to unbutton my shirt. I gave him a quick nod and he began fumbling with the buttons. As his hands touched my abdomen, he leaned in to kiss me again. It was a surreal feeling – his hands brushing against my bare skin as he kissed me deeply. My fingers tangled deeper in his hair as I felt his lips graze my shoulder. As his hands reached the button of my jeans, we heard a knock on the door. I wanted to kill whoever was ruining our moment.

"Wow, okay," I said getting up and buttoning my shirt.

Manav was sitting and smiling.

"What?" I asked.

"Nothing. Do you want to go see who is at the door?" he asked.

"Yeah, I am going," I said, fixing my hair and shirt before heading towards the door.

"Ma'am, your food," said a delivery guy. I looked at him with surprise.

"Babe, is that our food?" asked Manav.

"I haven't ordered any food," I said.

"Ma'am, your name is Riya, right?" he asked.

"Yeah," I said, holding the pack.

"Oh! Did you order food?" I asked and he nodded.

"Thanks," I told the delivery guy and shut the door.

"You did not tell me! What did you order?" I asked.

"I thought you were in bad mood so I'd ordered something to cheer you up," he said and took the packet from me and opened it up.

"Here, some cupcakes for you," he said and gave them to me.

"Wow, that's so kind of you, you didn't have to!" I said and hugged him.

As I bit into a cupcake, I couldn't believe I had found Manav. He was possibly trying to do everything that would make me feel better. It seemed unreal and hard to believe. How could someone do so much in such a short span of time?

"What's your angle here?" I blurted. *Oh god! I shouldn't have said it out loud.*

"Excuse me?" he seemed offended.

"No, wait! I mean, sorry. I didn't mean to," I blurted out, not really knowing what I wanted to say.

"What do you mean by angle?" he asked. "I am sorry but this is not cool Riya. You should let go of this negativity where you simply start questioning everything anyone does. It feels like you deliberately want to push people away. There are people who care for you! I think you should understand that by now."

"Ugh, Just please stop!" I said, furiously.

"What?" he said.

Suddenly, there was a sour taste in my mouth. I wanted Manav out of my house. He had no right to comment on my life like that.

"Okay, listen I am sorry. I shouldn't have spoken out of anger like that. Please understand that I am really trying here. You will have to allow me to care rather than being sceptical about everything," he said.

"Yeah... No, absolutely. I understand and I am sorry. Will you always have my back no matter what?" I asked.

"Of course, I will. Why do you ask?" he said.

"No. I mean I haven't had someone look out for me like this. Please be patient with me. All of this – is new and it is difficult for me to express myself appropriately. What I am trying to say is – I hope you don't run out of patience with me," I said.

"Yeah Riya, I understand but for that to happen, you will have to let me into your life. I cannot do anything to help you otherwise," he said.

"I know," I replied and gestured to him to eat the cupcake. "Sorry, I ruined your day," I said.

"No, please. You didn't," he said, biting into the cupcake.

"So, tell me how was your day?" he asked.

"Oh umm fine," I said, looking away, trying to change the topic.

"Okay. How did your meeting with your supervisor go?" he asked.

"It was okay, he suggested some changes and I'd have to work on that. I think he is just being mean. I have done everything according to the guidelines and have followed his suggestions to the 't' but he is just being an asshole," I said.

"Easy there, madam! He is your professor after all. Don't you think if you just listen to what he says, it'd be easier for you to be graded?" he asked.

"Don't you seem to know a little too much about PhD?" I asked, smirking.

"Okay Riya, I guess I should leave today. You have had a rough day," he said, getting up.

"I guess I should just take some time to myself to cool down and feel better."

Manav raised his eyebrows and said, "Sure, that makes sense."

"Yeah," I said, as he took his wallet.

"Bye Riya, please take care. I'll call you when you've calmed down a bit," he said.

"Calm? Excuse me?" I asked.

"Woah! Okay, I am going to go. Speak to you soon," he said and left without giving me a goodbye hug.

"Bye," I said as I shut the door.

'What the fuck Riya? What the actual fuck? Just pull yourself together and make sure you express the best of yourself to Manav. I thought to myself.

I was quite hungry and finished the rest of the cupcakes by myself and went to bed.

Perhaps I will feel better once I sleep.

It was 12 am and I just could not sleep. I tossed and turned, trying to find some peace.

I decided to eat something before sleeping again. I woke up feeling quite tired and I knew I had work to do. Soon after having my coffee and croissant, I went to bed. I woke up to a construction noise around 7:30 am. *People have to stop that.*

Perhaps having coffee and going straight to bed wasn't a good idea after all as I woke up feeling nauseous.

It was 10 am. I went in for a shower and looked at myself in the mirror.

"*You got this,*" I said firmly. I knew there were things I had to work on for the research before I could schedule my next visit to the professor. Perhaps a mini vacation would help too. For now, I had to gather myself and get into work.

I reached the coffee shop my usual time, 11:30 am.

"Hey Tina," I said as I entered the coffee shop.

"Hey! How are you?" she said, smiling.

"I am good. Can you please get me my regular. No croissant for now, please." I said.

"Okay sure," she said.

I sat at my regular table and noticed that Karan and Sachin weren't here yet.

I started working.

"Can I get a pen, Tina?" I asked a little loudly, as there was no one in the coffee shop. "Also, can you lower the temperature of the AC? It feels a little hot," I said.

"Oh, is it? It is at 16 already," she said.

"Oh! Maybe I am feeling hot because I just came from outside," I said, adjusting my shirt to feel better.

"Here, your pen!" she said.

"Thanks," I said. I began my work by listing down everything my professor had asked me to work on yesterday. He might have been a prick, but I will have to rework it anyway.

I realised the boys had still not come when the clock struck 1 pm. It was unusual for them to not be here.

With the interest I had developed in their lives, I felt like the neighbourhood aunty ready to get any information I could about their whereabouts. My thoughts were interrupted when a young man entered the coffee shop. He was a short, about 5'6" in mid-twenties, wearing pyjamas and a sports T shirt. He looked like a nerd with black rimmed spectacles with neatly done hair. He looked tense. He went to the counter and waited until Harry approached him.

I couldn't help myself from walking towards the counter. This looked suspicious and I knew I needed to be a part of it.

"Hello! Can I speak with the manager, please?" he asked.

"Sir, the Manager only visits once in a while. Please tell me what the issue is and I will try to help you out," Harry replied.

"I am Karan's friend. He comes here regularly with his brother. Have you seen him here today?" he asked.

"Umm you mean Karan Saxena?" Harry confirmed.

"Yeah, him. Did he come here today?" he asked.

"No sir. We haven't seen him or his brother Sachin come in today. Why sir, is everything okay?" asked Harry.

"Okay. Yes, yes… everything seems fine," he said and mumbled something to himself which seemed like an angry statement.

"Thanks for your time. Can you please keep it between us and not mention a word to anyone else?" he said, looking all serious.

"Sure, okay. Do you want me to inform you if I see him here?" asked Harry

"That's okay. I'd know, thanks," he said.

"Sir, wait! He left his mobile phone here," said Harry.

I looked at Harry in amusement, wondering about the series of events. Did he leave his phone by mistake?

"Oh yea?" the young man frowned. "Can you please give it to me?"

"Umm actually sorry sir. I'll give it to Sachin sir once he's here," said Harry.

The young man sized up Harry and left without another word.

"*Why was he looking for Karan? Where did Karan disappear? That young man seemed a little off in his actions and he was walking fast frantically. Something about him did not feel right,*" I thought to myself.

"Weird man!" Harry said out loud.

He finally noticed me and asked, "Hey! How can I help you?"

"Oh yea, I just came for another round of coffee," I said.

"Okay, I'll get it to your table. You are quite a quick coffee drinker!" he teased.

I gave him a smile and went back to my seat. I sat there patiently waiting for both boys to show up but there was no sight of them.

"All okay?" I asked Harry, meeting him at the counter.

"Yeah, it's just weird that this boy came looking for Karan. You know one of the brothers that come here?" he asked.

"Oh, yes! I have noticed them," I said. I didn't want to let him know that I knew much more about their personal lives than him – eavesdropping is not a good thing.

"I am sure it's nothing," he said and got back to his work. There were customers lining up to place their orders.

"I think we should look," I said, a bit loud without realising I wanted to just mention it to myself.

"Look for what?" he asked.

"Nothing, I am sure they must be out of town like they've been before," I said. Harry looked at me wondering how I'd know all of that.

"You knew them?" he asked.

"No not really, Just saw them here regularly like you guys do," I replied.

I couldn't help wondering about Sachin and Karan. It was evident that everyone knew that they were regulars here. But their whereabouts was a mystery.

I took out my phone to talk to Manav, but I realised we had left things weirdly between us. I did not know if he'd want to talk to me, given how I had behaved with him.

I went back to my writing and finished about 5 cups of coffee that day and was about to order another when Tina came over, "I know you are increasing my sale but I don't think drinking 6 cups of coffee is healthy. I believe you have had too much. Is everything okay with you?"

"Oh, umm… sorry, yes. It's just been a bit tense. By the way, Tina, how well do you know the Saxenas?" I asked.

"I mean everyone knew their family. They hail from Mumbai and have a house here. The brothers live with the caretaker here. The parents keep visiting Delhi on and off. They donate to a number of charities here in Delhi which is why they are popular in the area," she said.

"Oh, is it? Charities?" I said, with sarcasm in my tone. I somehow felt people with money were always showing off, instead of being genuine about things. Charities seemed like a façade to me.

"Yeah, we had a young man looking for Karan today. I have never seen him before. It is also strange that they did not come to the coffee house," she said. "Anyway, you please don't drink more." "*Why was she not concerned. Was it just me? Was I just thinking too much?*" I thought to myself.

"Thank you, Tina! Please get me the cheque," I said, feeling anxious and jittery, considering the excessive intake of caffeine.

I paid the bill and went back home. It felt better to continue working from home. I had to stop by for groceries.

When I stepped in the store, I saw Sachin with that young man who came looking for Karan in the coffee shop. They seemed to be fighting about something. I wanted to know more and decided to browse at their aisle, to eavesdrop on their conversation.

"I gave you one responsibility, Sarthak!" said Sachin, angrily.

"Listen, I know Sachin but Karan fought with me yesterday. I didn't know what to do but ask him to fuck off," replied Sarthak.

"You could have handled the situation better," said Sachin. He noticed me walking around the aisle.

"Hey, you are the girl from coffee house, aren't you?" he asked.

"Oh, hey!" I said, trying to sound surprised and continued, "Yes?"

"Yeah, my brother and I are regulars at that coffee shop," he said.

"Oh, alright, Yea I know, I have seen you guys around," I said.

"Have you seen my brother today?" he asked.

"I am not sure, I came around 11:30, so I don't really know," I said.

"Okay, cool," he said and got back to Sarthak.

I pretended to talk on the phone while he got back to talking to Sarthak.

"Sarthak you better sort this shit, I am not telling anything to Mom and Dad. You know Karan has done this before, but this time around we better be careful," said Sachin.

"Yeah I am on it," he said and as he said that, Sachin left.

"Weird brothers!" murmured Sarthak.

It felt like something had happened between Karan and Sarthak. As a result, Karan took off without informing them. It wasn't clear what exactly had happened. Sachin mentioned that Karan had run off before.

"*Cool*" I thought to myself.

I went and bought some groceries and decided to cook myself a meal. It felt like these young men were spoiled brats of a rich family. Everything gets served to them on a platter and they don't seem to know anything of the real world. They stunk of privilege.

Sachin's brother seemed to be missing and all he cared about was their parents coming to know about Karan's disappearance. I felt a little at peace knowing that at least, he was worried about this and will find his brother.

However, I did not trust Sarthak. The moment he had walked into the coffee house, I felt something off with him. He seemed way too suspicious. If he were so concerned about Karan, he would have told Harry at the coffee house to get back to him.

Although I was worried about Karan, I needed to get home and clear my mind. I paid for the groceries and got back to my apartment.

I made some Thai green curry and steamed rice for myself. It was quite tiring to cook for myself after a long day. I couldn't stop wondering what might have happened between those men and Karan.

I wondered if I could text Manav but decided against it.

It was quite difficult for me to sleep that night. I needed the next day to be as normal as it could be. I headed to the coffee shop but arrived there later than usual.

I reached around noon and saw Sarthak and Sachin there. He was sipping a cup of coffee and looked pretty normal.

We exchanged nods, acknowledging each other's presence. I wanted to keep my distance but stay close enough to know what was going on.

I went and sat in my seat.

"Getting your coffee," Tina said.

"Thank you," I said.

Sachin sat in silence, sipping coffee and scrolling through his phone. Harry hadn't arrived yet – I remembered he had to give Karan's phone to Sachin.

Just as that thought crossed my mind, Harry walked in.

"Oh, hi, Sachin sir. Karan sir left his phone here again!" Harry said.

"I've been waiting for you. Can you please give it to me?" Sachin replied.

"Yes, sir, just a moment," said Harry, heading to put his bag away. He soon returned with Karan's phone, which Sachin quickly took, looking rather anxious.

"Thanks, Harry," Sachin said. The phone seemed switched off, so Sachin moved to another seat and plugged it in to charge.

"C'mon, c'mon!" he muttered under his breath, impatiently waiting for the phone to power on. As soon as it did, he began frantically scrolling and opening apps left right.

"*Ugh! Sarthak!*" Sachin cursed, yanked the phone from the charger, and hurried out of the coffee shop.

"Thanks again, Harry," he called out on his way out.

Harry waved as Sachin left. I sat there, patiently drinking my coffee. Although I wanted to chase after Sachin to see where he was headed and what his next move was, I knew it would draw too much attention. After all, I was just a curious soul who really wanted to know what had happened.

I got back to my writing when my laptop chimed with a new email. It was my professor asking for more detailed notes on the changes he had suggested. It felt like there was so much to discuss and write about, but my mind was all over the place with this new mystery. On top of that, I had to focus on my analysis.

I had already gone through the literature review and was working on the analysis and hypothesis of the data. I quickly typed out a reply:

"*Hi Sir,*

I will work on all the changes you suggested earlier and get back to you at the earliest. Please let me know when we can meet to discuss this."

After sending the email, I shut my laptop and decided to take a break. I went for a walk around the block to clear my head, but before I got too far, I realised I'd left my phone at the coffee shop. Unlike Karan, I didn't want Harry to think I'd forgotten it, so I headed back.

I still didn't understand what was going on between Sarthak, Sachin, and how Karan was involved. Whatever it was, it didn't make sense. I wanted to meet Manav and confide in him.

"*Hey, meet at Elysian in half an hour?*" I texted Manav.

"*Hey, a little busy. Can't do today. How about tomorrow, provided you're in a better mood,*" he replied.

Wow, he was still upset about the day I'd acted weirdly with him.

"*Fine,*" I replied.

I decided to wait for Manav and continue working at the coffee shop. I decided to strike up a conversation with Harry. "Hey, Harry, any news about the boy – what was his name again?"

"Karan," he reminded me.

"Yeah, him," I replied.

"No, nothing that I know of. Looks like he must have run away or gone somewhere. You know how young people can be," Harry said.

"Yeah, I am sure, it's nothing to worry about," I replied.

"Even if it's something, their parents are high-profile. It'll get figured out soon," he added.

"Yeah? Aren't they in Bombay," I asked.

"Yeah, but everyone knows them around here," Harry said, glancing at two customers waiting to place an order. "Anyway, do you want something? I need to attend to the customers."

"Another latte, please," I said, and returned to my seat.

I was lost in my thoughts when I saw Manav enter the coffee shop.

"You?" I asked, surprised.

"Yeah, I was in the area so thought I'd drop by for a quick hello," he said, giving me a side hug before I could get up from my seat.

"Oh work? In this area?" I asked.

"Yeah," he replied without offering much details, and sat down across me.

"Okay, it's nice to see you," I replied, smiling halfway, comforted by his presence. I guess I need to see him.

"You too. Are you feeling better?" he asked, his fingers gently brushing mine. The slow movement of his hand trying to hold mine felt like a melody.

"Same old," I replied, distracted by his touch. Trying to focus, I asked, "Do you know the Saxenas?"

"The Saxenas from Mumbai?" he asked.

"Yeah, them," I said, curious.

"Yeah, what about them?" he asked.

"Nothing, just that a lot of people talk about them here," I said.

"They are big shots," he replied.

"Oh, okay. Rich people can be snobbish though, can't they?"

"Not that I know of," he said, then asked, "Anyway, why are you so interested in them?"

"Nothing. Do you want coffee?" I offered.

"No, I'm actually running late. I just thought I'd drop by for a quick minute," he said.

"That's sweet of you," I said, reaching out to hold his other hand, which was fiddling with a tissue on the table.

He smiled and held my hand. An electric shiver ran through my body. We were going to finish what we had started that day in my apartment. The vibes didn't lie.

"Okay, I'll leave now, but I'll see you tomorrow?" he asked.

"Yeah, okay. I'll text you," I replied.

"You're free, right?" he asked.

"Yeah, I'll be here, working on my research," I replied.

"Okay, that works. I'll drop you a text, and we'll plan something," Manav said, getting up to leave. He gave me a quick kiss on the forehead before heading out. I waved him goodbye. It felt like he genuinely had some work to attend to.

Harry arrived with my coffee, eyeing me with a hint of cheekiness.

"What?" I asked.

"Something is brewing," he teased.

I just shook my head in mild disbelief. "Please," I said, he smiled before walking away. Public displays of affection certainly catch people's attention, but I didn't want to dwell on it. I considered heading over to Karan and Sachin's place to see what was going on, but I held myself back, knowing it might lead to unnecessary questions. I also had to meet another professor to discuss the statistical tools and analysis I'd be using in my research.

It wasn't easy keeping my mind off all the drama, but I had no choice but to wait.

Another day passed, leaving me just as curious as before.

The next day was filled with clear anticipation, my anxiety growing as two days had passed without any update on the whole Karan situation. Like any other day, I planned to go to the coffee shop, but something in me knew I needed to break from the city's commotion. A day trip – a quick getaway – felt like the right move.

"*Do you want to get out of the city for a while today?*" I texted Manav.

"*What do you mean?*" he replied.

"*I mean a getaway. Maybe to a hotel with a pool? Just for a few hours?*" I suggested.

"*Okay, I am listening…*" he replied.

"*So?*" I pressed.

"*Let me see which hotel we can go to and spend a few hours alone,*" he texted back, clearly excited.

"*Ha-ha, let me know. I am up and about already,*" I replied.

"*It's done. I've booked a hotel. I have some work in the afternoon, but we can go now, chill for a bit, and get back. Does that work?*" he asked.

"*Couldn't be more excited. I could really use a few hours away from all the work and the drama.*" I texted back.

"*I'll be there soon to pick you up,*" said Manav.

"*Can't wait,*" I replied.

I quickly jumped in the shower, knowing that Manav, being the punctual person he was, would arrive on time. He was always prompt and hated when people didn't respect his time. Punctuality was something we connected on.

Even though it was a short getaway, I needed this escape. I deserved a bit of relaxation and peace of mind, and Manav seemed to understand that perfectly. I wasn't willing to let go of someone who agreed to this spontaneous plan without a second thought. I decided to wear something nice for a change – opting for a blue cotton dress with embroidered collars and quarter-length sleeves. The dress, which fell just below my knees, gave off a chic vibe. I tied my hair into a neat ponytail and packed a change of clothes, just in case we decided to swim.

While waiting for Manav to arrive, I made myself some coffee. It was earlier than my usual coffee time, but despite my excitement, a part of me felt anxious, and coffee seemed like the best remedy.

"*Reaching in 10*" a notification from Manav popped up.

"*See you,*" I replied.

I quickly downed my coffee, grabbed my bag, and took a last look in the mirror before locking up the house and heading downstairs. It had been ages since I'd taken a getaway, let alone a vacation. This was more of a mental detox for me.

As I reached the road, I saw Manav looking as radiant as ever, wearing a soft beige shirt and shades. It seemed like he'd recently gotten a haircut.

"Hey, you," I said as I slid into the front seat beside him.

"Hello, madam," he replied, giving me a slightly awkward hug due to the car's seat belt.

"So, where are we going?" I asked.

"Well, that's a surprise," he said with a grin.

"What? Come on, tell me! It was my plan, so you should at least clue me in. You know I don't like surprises," I said, placing my hand on his as he shifted gears.

"I will, just let us get on the road first," he responded, keeping the mystery alive.

I connected my phone to the car's Bluetooth to play some music.

"Do you want to stop by Elysian for your coffee?" he asked.

"Ah no, not really. Let's just go. I had coffee at home unless you want to stop?" I offered, even though I was eager to get going.

"No, let's head straight to the hotel," he said.

"Yeah, but please tell me. Not knowing makes me anxious, Manav," I said, a hint of hesitation in my voice.

"Let it go, Riya. Sometimes, you just have to let things be. Why do you always need to know and control everything?" he said, his tone firm. "Look, you wanted to go, and I didn't argue about this impromptu plan. So now, trust me to take us where we need to go, okay?"

His tone was so stern that my stubbornness paused. A part in me had no idea what to say more to get him to tell me where we were going.

"Okay if you say so," I replied, not entirely satisfied with the whole surprise element. Surprises aren't my thing; I was still trying to escape anxiety, but this surprise only added to it. Still, it was what it was.

"What are you thinking? Just relax. It is going to be amazing," he said. "We'll check in, have some fun, take a dip in the pool, and come back on time; it's a win-win," he said.

"Yeah, I am really looking forward to it," I replied, excited.

"But tell me, what made you plan the gateway?" he asked.

"Nothing, I was just done with all the pressure in the last few days," I said.

"Pressure?" he asked, turning down the volume of the music.

"Yeah, I mean just too much happiness in the world," I said.

"And that is a problem because?" he said, looking at me with surprise.

"Because everyone keeps pretending all the time," I said, trying to lighten the mood. Unsuccessfully, to say the least.

"Why are you thinking so much about others, Riya? I know things have been bitter in the past but the least you can do is appreciate whatever right is in the world," he said, smiling.

"True, okay let me volume up now," I replied, avoiding the conversation.

"Yes, madam," he replied.

"By the way, it's not a long drive so we will have ample time to chill at the hotel," he said.

I nodded, appreciating the effort he'd put in such a short notice.

After almost an hour's drive, we arrived at an ancient road lined with lights, old statues, and paintings in the street itself. As our car passed through a massive ancient gate, we were welcomed by hosts dressed in traditional Indian – it was the most unique scene I had seen in a long time. The sign read "The Royal Palace." I'd heard about this place but never been here. It was an hour's drive from Delhi and located in the woods, away from the hustle and bustle of the city. It was amazing how a fifteen-minute stretch could transport you to a completely different experience.

"Welcome! Here's to our first of many," Manav said, smiling.

"Wow," I thought to myself.

I smiled at Manav's statement and said, "It looks amazing."

I was a little hesitant and anxious; as an introvert, stepping out of my comfort zone wasn't easy, but this was exciting. Manav handed the car to the valet, and we both got out to check in. Even though we weren't staying overnight, it felt worth the visit.

"Welcome ma'am ,Welcome Sir," greeted the manager, who was standing close to the reception.

"You relax; I'll get our room keys," Manav said.

"Okay, sure" I replied, heading to a sofa in the lobby.

Next to me was a table with refreshment, mainly mocktails. I picked one up and took a sip. The hotel was quiet but had soft music playing in the background.

I had never imagined I'd enjoy myself as much as I was, in that moment. My lack of social skills had always kept me away from experiences like this. Back in school, I rarely joined trips because I was too hesitant, too uneasy around crowds. I struggled with interaction, never quite able to express myself.

So, this mini-getaway meant more to me than anyone could possibly understand.

"So, we have our keys – ready to go?" Manav asked, standing there, making me nearly swoon with his charm.

"Of course," I said, taking his hand as we headed to the elevator.

As we entered our room, I couldn't believe my eyes – there was a private pool just for us. It was the perfect romantic escape.

"Wow, this is amazing," I exclaimed, my excitement unmistakable. I couldn't stop smiling, though a small part of me felt a creeping fear of the unknown.

"I know, right? This was the surprise I couldn't wait to show you. I hope it was worth the wait," Manav said, pulling me close by the waist.

"Of course, I mentioned a pool, and you got a pool in the room," I said, relaxing into his embrace. He turned me around to face him, brushing a strand of hair behind my ear. He undid my ponytail, letting my hair fall loose. With one hand in my hair and the other gently cupping my face, he leaned in and kissed me. I let my guard down and kissed him back. It was a kiss filled with passion and calm – a moment that felt surreal.

I pulled back slightly, looking him in his eyes, "You're amazing," I whispered.

"And you stopped kissing me just to tell me that? I know I am amazing," he teased.

"Okay, let me just go change. I don't want to waste any time – I'm jumping straight into that pool," I said, smiling.

"Sure, let me use the washroom. You go ahead, and I'll join you soon," he replied.

I grabbed my bag and quickly changed into a black swimsuit that perfectly matched the room's aesthetic. It felt like I deserved this break, like I was meant to experience this amazing hotel and this mini vacation. I shook my head, gave myself a big smile and jumped into the pool.

"Wow, *this is amazing,*" I thought to myself, feeling pure joy. But just a few minutes into my swim, Manav's phone started ringing. He was still in the washroom, and his phone was charging nearby.

"Manav, your phone!" I shouted, hoping he'd hear me. There was no response, from Manav, and the phone eventually stopped ringing. I continued to play around in the pool, but the phone began ringing again. I was about to get out when Manav finally emerged out of the washroom.

"Your phone's been ringing non-stop," I told him.

"Oh, looks like I have a lot of missed calls," he said, glancing at the screen.

"Who is it? Is everything okay?" I asked, seeing Manav's eyebrows go up as he scrolled his phone

"Just a moment," he said, walking out of the room to take a call.

As I floated in the pool, I couldn't shake the feeling that something was wrong. The energy in the room had shifted, and Manav leaving to take the call felt strange. He returned a few moments later, his expression had changed.

"Listen we need to leave immediately. Please change, and let's go," he said urgently.

"Leave? What do you mean? We just got here, Manav. What happened?" I asked, my voice mixed with confusion and frustration.

"Riya, please do not argue. There's an urgent issue at my Dad's work, and I have to be there," he replied, avoiding details.

"We just got here. Why do you always have to work, babe? Can't your dad handle whatever it is?" I asked with disappointment in my eyes and tone.

"You please need to understand, Riya. Please, babe, let's just go," he pleaded, rushing to change into his clothes. "If you want to stay, I can leave and pick you up tomorrow."

"No, that's not necessary. I do not need your favour," I blurted, still in the pool, trying to process what was happening.

"Riya? Favour? Please, tell me what you want to do. Will you please change?" he asked, his voice filled with urgency.

"*What has happened to this man?*" I thought to myself, finally getting out of the pool.

Manav emerged from the washroom within seconds, fully dressed. "Babe, let's go," he said, his voice tight.

"First, tell me what happened," I insisted, stubbornly holding my ground.

"There's been a murder! Happy now?" he blurted out.

"What?" I gasped, immediately jumping out of the pool, "A murder? Whose? What are you saying?"

"I can't give you more details for now, Riya, but please, let's just go," he urged.

"Okay," I replied, shaken. I quickly changed and tried to dry my hair but the dryer fell out of my hands!

"Riya are you all right?" I heard Manav's voice.

"Ah, yeah," I said, picking up the dryer.

A murder! I thought to myself! I tied my hair wet and packed my wet swimsuit into a polybag.

"Sorry, can you hand me my bag," I called, sticking my arm out of the washroom.

Manav immediately handed it to me.

"Here," he said.

I stuffed the polybag into my tote after getting out of the washroom.

"Let's go," I said, and we left the room without anther word. The elevator ride was silent, tension hanging heavy in the air. I was furious at the world for ruining what would have been an amazing moment, but murder was serious. Manav hadn't given me any details, but I needed to find out what was going on – and how he was involved.

We got into the car, and Manav started the engine, his anxiety showing, in the way he gripped the wheel.

"Calm down! Take it slow," I said.

"I'm sorry. It's just that it's only 12 pm, and we're already leaving. I'll drop you at the coffee shop. I cannot say much now, but I promise I'll tell you more when I know," he said, his voice strained.

"Yeah, that's okay," I replied, still trying to grasp the intensity of the situation. "But you know who's been murdered, don't you?" I asked.

Manav glanced at me but said nothing. The silence between us was thick with tension, and my curiosity and anger were battling for dominance.

The 45-minute drive back was quiet, interrupted only by Manav's phone ringing again and again, calls he didn't answer.

"I'll drop you at Elysian?" he asked.

"Umm, okay, that'd be nice," I said, not knowing what else to do. I thought maybe the familiar environment would help calm my nerves.

We arrived at the coffee shop, and Manav pulled over a few blocks away.

"Okay, you go in, and I'll call you soon," he said.

"Okay, you call me when you know more," I said as I got out of the car.

"Bye," he said, and drove off.

I entered the coffee shop, and immediately, I sensed something was off. The usual murmur was subdued. Sachin was there, walking hither and thither in the coffee shop.

I took my regular seat, noticing that the usual warmth was absent.

Harry and Tina were there, but they seemed distant, their expressions sombre.

"Hey Tina," I greeted her.

"Hi, I'll get your coffee," she said, with a dim light and mood.

She brought the coffee over, placed it in front of me, and walked away. The vibe of different – this wasn't the usual Elysian Coffee House. I glanced over at Sachin, wondering about Karan. Sachin remained silent, focused on his phone.

"Tina?" I called out.

"Yeah?" she replied, coming over.

"Can you please come here?" I asked

Tina finished serving another table and then came over to me. "Yeah, Riya?" she asked.

"Listen, what is going on? Why is everyone so down?" I asked, confused.

"You don't know?" she asked, her voice almost a whisper.

"Don't know what?" I asked, my heart sinking.

"Karan's been murdered," she said.

Silence. I felt the world around me stop, unable to process what I'd just heard.

"What?" I asked, needing to hear it again to believe it.

"Karan. Remember, Sachin's brother? He was found dead today and it looks like a murder," she said.

This was beyond anything I could have imagined. My body went numb, my mind reeling. I simply couldn't fathom what had just happened.

"Yeah, the town knows, even though they're trying to keep it low-key," she tried to whisper, for Sachin, but failed miserably. Sachin's head turned towards us. He sized us up and then got up to leave the café.

My body felt numb, and the café, once my safe haven, now felt suffocating. Karan and Sachin had become part of my routine, and this sudden news had shaken me to the core. My hands trembled as I tried to sip my coffee. I quickly pulled out my phone to text Manav.

"*It was Karan, right?*" I typed, my fingers unsteady.

"*I'll call you in a bit. There's a lot going on right now,*" he replied.

"*K,*" I texted back. He was obviously occupied. I hoped he would confide in me, that he trusted me enough to share the details, but the protector in me wanted to help Sachin too. I had to know what happened. Karan seemed like an amazing child with a bright future. To have seen him just a few days and now hear that he was murdered – it was too much to process.

Chapter 6

Find the Killer

The day of the murder discovery was the hardest to endure. The gossip spread like wildfire, becoming the talk of the town. The news still hadn't covered it yet. I packed my things and went home, feeling lost, and uncertain of what to do. It felt like a part of my life had crumbled, yet the killer was still out there.

I couldn't shake the feeling that I had to tell Manav what I knew.

"*Listen we need to talk,*" I texted him.

"*About what?*" he immediately replied.

"*The murder. I think I can help. I might know something,*" I typed, trying to sound confident.

"*What do you mean?*" he asked

"*Let's meet and discuss,*" I replied.

"*Okay. I need some time. I'll be there,*" he said.

"*Okay. I am home. Come whenever,*" I texted back, my mind racing.

I knew something was off when Karan disappeared. I had overheard enough conversations between Sachin and Karan to sense some underlying tension – was it jealousy, or something more sinister? And Sarthak, who had appeared out of nowhere in Karan's life, seemed to have ulterior motives. His body language had made me uncomfortable, and their conversation that day had raised too many red flags. If I could convince Manav to trust me, maybe I could help solve this. Karan deserved justice.

I went home and took a long shower, trying to wash away the anxiety that had taken hold of me. My thoughts spiralled – should I just stay silent and let things play out? Would Manav even need my help? I kept mumbling these questions to myself, feeling utterly lost.

Maybe a walk would clear my head. I decided to step out and go out for a walk. It felt like it was difficult to breathe. I wandered aimlessly around Hauz Khas, not knowing where I was headed. The streets were unusually quiet, but the tension in the air was palpable. Police presence was heavy, adding to the unease. I walked through the streets, feeling the weight of the situation.

At one point, the area was sealed off. From a distance, I saw Manav talking to someone in a suit – someone who seemed connected to the investigation.

As our eyes met, Manav gestured at me with an expression that clearly said, "What the hell are you doing here?"

I realized, going any further would draw attention and that wouldn't be good for Manav. So I decided to head home and wait for Manav there.

I wondered if Karan's parents were with the policemen. I wanted to know more about how he was murdered and how the investigation was progressing. For now, going home would be the best idea.

As I crossed the cafe, I saw Sachin engrossed in his phone, mumbling and typing frantically. He seemed anxious and facial expressions were not the best. Why was he standing outside the coffee house?

I impatiently waited for Manav to come home. I wanted to know more but also wanted to see if I could help. I knew the detectives would do their job but perhaps I could point them in the right direction.

I went home and gulped a glass of water. I went inside my bedroom and took a nap. It had been an exhausting day. From a glimpse of a perfect staycation to news of a bright child being murdered – it became one of the scariest days of my life. I had felt deep happiness after such a long time but even that was snatched away, and how! I wanted everything to get over and just wanted to spend time with Manav, planning our future.

I guess I had to solve the mystery myself, to get it done faster! I had to add two and two together to find the killer. Who did Karan have issues with? It must be Sarthak. He was the one who saw him last. Was it possible for his parents to be involved too? I didn't realize when I fell asleep but I woke up to my phone ring.

"*Hey, I've been knocking,*" Manav's message flashed on the screen.

"*Oh,*" I said and woke up feeling very low. I felt tired as it felt like we were in the middle of the night – although, it was just 9 pm. I went to the washroom and quickly splashed some water on my face to freshen up a bit. I looked like a mess.

"Hey," I said opening the door for Manav to come in.

"Hey, how are you?" he replied, side-hugging me.

"I am good. Come sit," I guided him to the sofa, "Should I order some food for you? You have been out the whole time."

"I don't mind a little bit of salad. It's been a weird day," he said.

"I am sure. I was shocked to hear about Karan as well," I replied.

"Yeah, the entire town is in shock, nobody knows what happened. This case has to be discreet because of the parties involved," he replied.

"Exactly, how are you related to this case, Manav?" I asked. He looked at his phone and replied to a few texts. It was evident that his mind was still in the investigation.

"Manav?" I said.

"Yeah, I have connections here. I help the officers because of my work in the cybercrime department," he replied. "Also…," he was about to say something but his phone kept buzzing because of constant messages.

"Just a minute, okay?" he said and got up to make a call.

"Yeah, no worries," I said.

Even though the incessant calls felt annoying, I knew they were important. Manav took the call and completed it in a few minutes.

"Hey, sorry, you know a lot is going on. I am trying to keep everything under control. We are under a lot of pressure and it has to be kept away from the media," he said, readjusting to sit closer to me on the sofa.

"I know, I completely agree. It is quite difficult to investigate while keeping everything under wraps," I said.

"Yes, anyway, you said you have some information on this case. What is it that you know?" he asked.

"Oh yea, I am not even sure if it's relevant but it's something regarding the brothers," I said.

"No please, nothing is irrelevant. Please tell me everything you know. I am sure it will help us," he said.

"Okay. Sachin and Karan were regulars at the coffee shop I go to. As I used to be there almost every time, I overheard many of their conversations. It sounded a bit fishy," I said.

"What do you mean, fishy?" he asked.

"I mean the other day, I overheard Karan talking about a Europe trip. He was travelling with his parents. Sachin was jealous of that trip because he wasn't going with them. In most of the conversations, Sachin used to complain about their parents being partial towards Karan," I said.

"But that's normal between siblings, right?" he asked.

"No, how is it normal? Karan was autistic, you know that right?" I asked.

"Everyone knew," he said

"Oh, okay. Naturally, their parents cared extra for Karan because of that, and Sachin was not appreciated enough," I replied.

"I think this is too far an assessment," he said.

"I am telling you, there was something off about it all," I said, uncomfortable with how normally he treated my analysis.

"Okay, I hear you and anyway, everyone attached to him will be questioned including his parents," he said, calmly.

"Oh yeah, for sure," I said.

"Since when did you become Sherlock?" he asked, with a slight smile.

"No, I am no detective at all. I feel invested because I saw Karan and Sachin almost every day. I think I can help more if you let me," I said.

"Okay, madam. I am all ears. What else do you have up your sleeve?" he asked, folding his legs on the sofa, getting more comfortable.

"I suspect their friend, Sarthak," I said.

"Sarthak?" he asked, frowning at the unfamiliar name.

"Yeah, Sarthak. He is Karan and Sachin's friend and I saw him when Karan went missing. I overheard Sachin and Sarthak talk about how Karan went missing because Sarthak argued with him. Sachin was livid about how Karan was nowhere to be found, and he cursed Sarthak as well. Sarthak seemed relaxed though as Karan missing was a normal thing. Everything was fishy about the way they behaved that day," I said.

"I am sure we'll get to the bottom of this once we get more details. Sarthak seems interesting," he said.

"Yeah," I said. I hoped he would take me seriously and interrogate these two based on my narration. It still bothered me that I didn't know how Manav was related to the case. How is cybercrime involved in this? I would be clueless about this until Manav divulged more information – or maybe I should do my own digging. I could help in getting more leads.

"Hey, you coming?" asked Manav. He was waiting for the salad.

"Yeah," I said and carried two plates to him for dinner.

"We will figure this out," he said, chewing his lettuce.

"I am sure. Don't worry, I am sure the culprit will be out soon," I replied.

We had our dinner in silence as I didn't want to talk more about the case with him. He seemed already stressed about it, asking about it again and again will just agitate him.

"I'll leave in a bit," he said, after finishing dinner. He cleaned his plate and lay on the sofa with me. Our legs were intertwined in each other's, as we talked about our favourite movies and how we enjoyed different characters. It was probably the calm moment I needed in the middle of the chaos that it was.

"Call me if you need my help. Please talk to Sachin and Sarthak," I said as Manav got up to leave.

"Of course," he said and left, without hugging me.

Chapter 7
Interrogation - Day 1

Sachin - POV

It had been two days since the news of Karan, my brother's murder broke. I was asked to appear at the police station for questioning. My phone had been taken into custody probably because they needed to check our message exchanges. I wasn't sure why but it felt like the police were considering me as one of the suspects. At this moment, nothing made sense.

As I entered the investigation room, I noticed the policemen interrogating me.

"Why am I here?" I asked the young man who was sitting beside an older guy, who seemed much senior. "My brother has been murdered and instead of letting me process this and find the real killer, you are questioning me!" I snapped, unable to control my anger.

"You need to calm down, sir," the young man murmured.

How dare he? Does he even understand my feelings? I glared at him. "Who are you?" I demanded. "I feel like I have seen you," I said, noticing his features.

"Not relevant here sir. Please cooperate with us. We know it has been a nightmare. I request you cooperate with us. We want to ensure that Karan's murderer is caught," he said. "My name is Manav and this is Mr. Das," he said.

"Okay, thank you," I said, calming down a bit, and continued, "Ask what you want to ask."

"How was your relationship with Karan?" asked Mr. Das, the senior official.

"I loved my brother. He has been so kind to me," I replied.

"Do you reciprocate the sentiment? Did it not bother you that he was autistic?" asked Manav.

"Of course not, why would it? Like any other siblings, we had fought and made up. Karan had a difficult childhood but he grew up to be an amazing child. We'd often forget that he had autism," I replied, confidently.

"Okay but then, would you say that you envy him?" asked Manav

"Envy? Why?" I asked.

"How is your relationship with your parents? Do you think that they treat you differently?" he asked.

"No, they… love us both… equally," I said, my voice sounding shaky.

"Why are you hesitating?" asked Mr. Das.

"No, I am not," I answered. I started feeling uncomfortable in this whole setup. Either it was the entire atmosphere or it was genuinely getting too hot in the room.

"Okay, Sachin, Who do you stay with in Delhi?" asked Mr. Das.

"Karan and I used to live with Samita Aunty and Ramesh *Bhaiya*. They are our caretakers," I said.

"Where were they when Karan disappeared?" he asked.

"They were at home, obviously," I said.

"Obviously?" he mocked.

"Yeah," I said.

"Why did they not look for Karan? Why were the police not informed about his disappearance earlier?" he asked.

"Can I please get some water?" I asked.

"Sure," said Manav, and got up to get water. He was smiling.

"Here you go," said Manav, handing the glass of water over to me.

"Thanks," I said and chugged it down my throat.

"So, tell me Sachin, why did you not inform anyone of Karan's disappearance?" asked Mr. Das.

"Sir, Karan had run away before as well. He does that whenever he is upset. I thought he would come back," I said.

"Why was he upset? Where were you?" he asked.

"He wasn't upset. The last time I saw him was in the coffee house where I left him," I said.

"But, earlier, you said that he was upset," he said.

"He might have been upset because of the fight he had with my friend," I said.

"Please tell us more," he asked.

"Karan did not approve of the way Sarthak and I were pursuing a girl," I said, getting worked up.

Manav looked up, his eyes gleaming – this was what they needed.

"Okay, so what? It was just a fight! I wanted this girl to come with me for a trip. Karan thought I had no intention of getting serious so he was pissed at us. Sarthak had already dated her, so he was just giving me some advice," I said.

"He also messaged Sarthak that he would stop talking to him, if he did not tell Amisha of my intentions. He threatened to talk to Amisha and show her the conversation between Sarthak and me," I replied.

"What were your intentions, Sachin?" Manav asked.

"How is this relevant for fuck's sake?" I said, getting annoyed and irritated at this whole interrogation.

"Lower your voice, please. There are cameras here," he said and waved his hand towards the camera.

"I am sorry. I need my lawyer. You cannot force me into an interrogation like this," I said, confidently and got up to leave.

"We'll meet you soon, Mr. Sachin," said Mr. Das.

"Sure," I said and walked out of the door.

POV: Sarthak

"Hello, Sarthak! How are you? I am Manav and this is Mr. Das."

"Hello, Sir," I replied, eyeing Mr. Das.

"You know why you are here, don't you?" asked Mr. Das. Manav stepped out, looking at his phone as he was getting numerous back to back calls.

"I am aware sir," I said, sobbing.

"Okay, please tell me how did you know Karan?" asked Mr. Das.

"I cannot believe he is gone and no longer chilling with me," I said and continued, "I knew Karan from college. We were together in the same class. He was a dear friend, I used to hang out with him and his brother Sachin."

"Exactly what happened between you and Karan a few days ago, Sarthak?" he asked.

"Sir, I fought with him, the last time I saw him. He had threatened to talk to a girl Sachin liked. He liked her too, Sir. He was just worried that something would happen between them when he was in Europe. After the argument, he ran away from my apartment. I haven't seen him since. I tried looking for him but it wasn't fruitful," I replied.

All I could think was about getting out of that room.

"Didn't you start searching for him much later? Why?" said Manav, waving his hand in front of my eyes.

"Karan tends to get upset about minor things and there's nothing we can do about it. We fought about the same thing once and he vanished. He did not come home for a day, because he was so upset. He stayed the night at a hotel. He's a little sensitive but we did not know it'd affect him so much this time," I said.

"Why do you think it affected him so much?" Manav asked.

"Sir, in the past Sachin has had a difference with that girl and a fight, which Karan was quite against. Sachin kept dating her and hated Karan for liking her too. The brothers always fought about her before. I was merely helping Karan get some perspective," I said.

"Perspective?"

"I simply told him how he has to forget about her and not bother about what Sachin was doing. After all, Sachin has been there for Karan most of the time," I said.

"And then you decided to gaslight them and murder him," said Manav.

"Excuse me?" I said, in shock, and continued, "how can you even say that?"

"What did Sachin do or what was he planning to do?" he asked.

"Sir, Sachin had planned to take Amisha on a vacation, once Karan went to Europe. He thought he'd charm her into being with him," I said, a little embarrassed to share the details.

"When did you last meet or text him?" he asked.

"Why were you so interested in stopping Karan? What did you have to do with it?" he asked.

"I just didn't want them to fight. I hadn't seen Sachin feel so strongly about anyone which is why I advised Karan to step back," I said.

"After this, Karan disappeared, didn't he?" he asked.

"So I've heard," I said.

"Where were you on the day of the murder?" he asked.

"I was at home," he said.

"But I thought you were looking for Karan, weren't you?" he asked.

"I mean, when the news of the murder broke, I was at home," I said, "but before that, I was looking for Karan," I said, feeling breathless.

"Why do you look scared, Sarthak?" asked Manav.

"It's just my first interrogation. Believe me, Sir. I did not murder Karan. I was just helping the brothers about the girl," I said.

Manav handed me a glass of water.

"Thank you," I said. I was unable to breathe and I couldn't wait for the interrogation to get over.

"Sarthak, thank you for your time. We'll be in touch again," he said. "Oh! By the way, we do have your phone data in our possession," Manav smiled at me. It did not feel good and I almost puked.

Present day

I missed Manav. I was curious as to what was happening with the case. I knew interrogations were in progress but anxious to know the outcome. I had worked quite a lot, the day I did not meet Manav. I was able to finish drafting all the changes my professor had asked me to make.

I spent the rest of the evening listening to music. Manav was supposed to come home in a few minutes. And to no one's surprise, he was at the door with a bouquet of flowers in his hand.

"Oh wow," I said, as I welcomed him in.

"Yes, for being patient," he said.

"Come, have a seat, I have made some pasta for you," I giggled and gave him a peck on his cheek.

"Oh wow, why the special treatment?" he asked, sitting down on the couch.

"Well, didn't you get me flowers?" I said.

He smiled and turned on the TV. I put some pasta in the bowl and brought it for him.

"Here you go," I said, passing him the plate and fork.

"It smells heavenly. I am sure it'd be delicious," he said, trying a bite of the pasta. "Oh yum!" he exclaimed.

"Thank you, I appreciate it," I said. "How have you been, babe? I'm sure you must have had some heavy work days?" I asked, rubbing his back.

"Yeah, it's been a lot of work lately. Honestly I am fatigued," he replied.

"I am sure, Manav. Please do let me know if I can help you in any way," I said.

He smiled and nodded, eating his pasta.

"So babe, what is happening with Karan's case? Do they have some leads?"

"I know you are concerned Riya, but I don't want to talk about it," he said.

"I told you I overheard conversations and it all gave it away," I insisted on continuing. But his continued silence said a lot.

"He never should have walked out that day," I said.

"Who?" he asked.

"I saw Karan leave from the coffee house the other day and I think he went missing after that," I said.

"Yeah, so I've heard," he said.

"But what has the team gathered from the investigations so far?" I asked.

"This is confidential, but I assure you they are working on the tips and leads you provided," he replied, eating quite quickly.

"What's the rush?" I asked.

"Nothing, I just realized I need to do something real quick," he said.

"What, you've just come so please relax and eat patiently," I said, putting my hand on his shoulder.

"Yeah, don't worry, I will. I am sorry, I'll eat slowly," he said and eased down a bit.

It felt like he was lost in his thoughts figuring something out. I gave him a kiss on his head.

"Tell me, have you guys found a murder weapon?" I asked.

"Yes, we did," he said.

"What? Really? I did not know about it," I said and continued, "So what weapon was it? I am dying to know!"

"Riya?" he said, disappointed.

"I am sorry! I am sorry, I am just curious. It drives me crazy when I don't know what is happening," I replied, lying down on the sofa.

"I understand, such are murder mysteries," he said, smiling, and continued, "Tell me, how is your thesis going?"

"Same old, same old," I replied.

"Yeah? You didn't go back to meet your professor after the last time?" he asked.

"Na, we've discussed meeting but haven't fixed a date yet. I have worked on the changes he suggested and I think I should meet him real soon," I replied.

"That's great. I hope you get to this real soon and finish everything," he said.

"I am indeed quite excited about it," I replied.

After Manav left, I decided to step out for a walk. I put on my sports shoes and went out for a walk. I felt this whole murder mystery had taken up a lot of space in my head too.

I moved past Elysian Coffee House, and my phone rang with a text notification.

"*What are you doing? I miss you,*" said Manav.

"*Already?*" I asked.

"*Yeah, just been stressful few days. I wish I could spend the night at yours,*" he said.

"*Me too. I just am going to sleep soon,*" I replied.

"*Ah okay, then I won't keep you awake, my love,*" he texted.

"*I'll see you soon. Perhaps tomorrow?*" I texted back.

"*Yeah, we'll try to,*" he texted.

"*See you, good night,*" I replied.

He sent a smile emoji and I put my phone back in my pocket. Manav seemed to be completely smitten with me. I hope we get some time alone together in the coming future.

I walked and walked until I was tired and mentally slightly free, however, the case details kept bothering me and I had to know the details of the killer, the description, the murder weapon, and everything.

I headed back home and as I reached the coffee house, I saw Sachin with two elderly-looking people. They might be his parents – Manav had told me that they had landed on the day the investigation began and were cooperating well with the investigation.

The mother was short and thick-haired, well dressed, lean built, and about 5'6" inches tall. She wore a beige kurta set. Something about her eyes caught my attention. They were seemingly swollen yet she carried herself with grace. The gentleman on the other hand was wearing a *kurta* and *kohlapuri sandals.* He was about six feet tall, had curly hair, specs on his eyes, and seemed very lost. He was of average build and it seemed like he worked out to maintain his physique.

I do not know why but I immediately smiled.

They smiled back.

I stopped and said, "I am sorry. I heard about what happened. Are you guys okay?"

"What do you expect?" said Sachin.

"How did you know Karan?" asked the lady and continued, "I am his mother."

"Oh, I didn't know him. I recently moved here and we just worked from the same coffee house, that's all," I replied.

"He was a beautiful child. I loved him to bits," she said, sobbing. The gentleman in brown kept his hand on her shoulder to console her.

"I am sure he was beautiful. Sometimes, nothing is in our control. I hope your family finds peace and strength to deal with this loss," I said.

They both nodded and started walking at a slow pace.

I had to tell Manav that I saw them out in the open.

"*Hey,*" I texted.

"*You haven't slept yet?*" he immediately replied, as if he was on his phone.

"*Oh, couldn't sleep. I just stepped out and guess who I bumped into!*" I texted back.

"*Who?*" said the text.

"*I met Sachin.*" I texted.

"*Oh, that is strange.*" he replied.

"*Sachin had no remorse, no guilt, no sadness, on his face, Manav,*" I replied, typing pretty fast. I could feel myself getting angry.

"*Calm down. There is no evidence about him being a murderer. They cannot arrest anyone without that. Also, he has a lawyer now, which has become slightly tricky. But I am sure they are close to cracking the case,*" he texted.

"*Yeah? Are they?*" I texted.

"*Yes, now go to sleep. I guess I will take your help after all,*" he replied.

Interrogation Day 2

Manav's POV

Mrs. Saxena

"It has been a tiring week, Madam. I hope you'll cooperate," said Mr. Das.

"Did I ever refuse?" she said.

"Okay. Please tell us where were you on the day Karan went missing?" he asked.

"We were in Mumbai. We had to take a flight to Delhi to meet Karan and Sachin. We planned to travel to Europe, but, unfortunately, it all...," she couldn't finish the sentence and started crying.

"Ma'am, I am sorry, please have some water," I said and handed over a glass of water to her.

"Mrs. Saxena, I know this is a difficult conversation but we'd appreciate it if you could please answer us. It will help us expedite the process and find the truth," I said, assuring and reaffirming her to be patient.

"Yeah, sorry," she said, wiping her tears and continued, "I loved him so much. He was my child and it's just unimaginable that he is murdered! He had never been in a fight. He was righteous, clear-headed, and always up for the right thing. I don't know what happened and who hated my child so much to have him killed."

"We understand that madam. Can you describe your relationship with him? How close were you? Who did he rely on? Who did he reach out to when things were bad?" I asked.

"He was quite close to his father. He has always been. He and I shared a good bond. We loved each other but when it came to sharing his feelings and emotions, he relied on his dad. Although, quite recently we rekindled our relationship as well," she replied.

"What changed, when you said he became close to you?" asked Mr. Das.

"Sachin and Karan were fighting and I just intervened in one of their fights. I took Karan's side, helped the boys solve their differences, and suggested this trip," she said.

"Ma'am, why did you only want to take Karan on this trip?" I asked

"I just thought it'd be a change for him," she said.

"Okay and why did you not consider taking Sachin on this trip?" I asked.

"What are you implying?" she asked, a bit furious. "Do you think I discriminate between my children?"

"We are not saying that. Please try to understand that our job is to ask as many questions as possible to find out the truth," I replied.

"Sachin had work to do. My intention was never to hurt him. I just wanted Karan to go and enjoy this trip for himself and feel important," she said, trying to calm herself down.

"So you are admitting that Sachin felt hurt?" I pointed out.

"No, I did not mean that," she said, shuddering and feeling frustrated.

"Then what is it that you want to say, ma'am?" I asked.

"No, I mean of course children feel bad. Although, I don't think this is relevant here," she said.

"No ma'am, every detail matters," I said, with a sigh. "How would you describe Karan and Sachin's relationship before Karan disappeared?"

"Nothing, Sachin was happy for Karan. He felt bad that he couldn't join but it never bothered him to the extent that he would kill Karan, I'd never let that happen," she said.

"But we did not accuse Sachin of anything," said Mr. Das.

"You are implying that Sachin is responsible. I love them both, you can ask their dad," she said.

"How long have you been married to Mr. Saxena?" I asked.

"About thirty years now," she said.

"Was it an arranged setup or love, ma'am?" I asked.

"It was an arranged marriage," she said. "We...," she stopped.

"We?" asked Mr. Das.

"We fell in love, so you can call it whatever you want to call it," she replied.

"Can you please tell us about your conversation with Sachin a few days ago?" I asked.

"I just told him that he should not go now, and plan a trip later," she said but panicked as she realized what her words would imply.

"Enough. I am done here. From now on, I would like to have my lawyers with me when I speak with you. My son is dead and all you care about is my marriage and relationship," she said.

"Alright Ma'am," I said and smiled.

She left in haste and anger, with tears in her eyes.

"I don't understand this family. They are quite complicated," said Mr. Das.

"I know, right? I feel they are hiding something. They seem quite suspicious. We need to dig deeper," I said.

"Yes, let's call Mr. Saxena in for questioning," said Mr. Das.

"Yeah, hopefully we get some lead from him," I said.

Mr. Saxena

"Hello Mr. Saxena, please have a seat," I said.

"Hi, thank you," he said, sobbing. His lawyer was with him and he insisted to talk but Mr. Saxena took the lead.

"How are you, Sir?" I asked.

"How do you imagine?" he asked.

"I am sorry for your loss, Mr. Saxena. I am aware that it is a terrible time for your family, but I would appreciate it if you answer my questions diligently. It will help us find out who killed your son," I said.

"Sure, I just want that person to be caught soon," he replied.

"Yes, sir. How was your relationship with Karan?" I asked.

"It was not great at first, but with time we got a lot closer. Karan had a different view of the world. I didn't always agree but in time, the differences blurred and we got closer," he replied.

"Why was it strained at first?" I asked.

"Well, he was closer to his mother. She was quite protective of him. He used to rarely speak with anyone else. It is quite normal for autistic kids to distance themselves from people," he said.

"Did you notice a change in his behaviour in the last few days?" I asked.

"He was a bit stressed. He was fighting with Sachin about something and he has also preparing for the Europe trip," he said.

"Do you know why they were fighting?" I asked.

"I am not sure, he never told me but they are siblings. I dismissed it as a regular fight. It didn't look like anything of great concern," he said. His lawyer got up to speak but Mr. Saxena gestured to him to keep sitting.

"All right. Where were you when Karan went missing?" I asked.

"I was actually at a conference in Hyderabad but my wife and I had planned to come to Delhi to take Karan for his vacation," he said.

"Did you contact him in the past few days?" I asked.

"Just a few regular text exchanges and phone calls about his well-being and we met on and off to discuss about our trip to Europe," he said.

"But did you notice any change? Anything you can help with in this case?"

"He was just quiet and frustrated. I remember that he called me about two days before he went missing. He said he missed us," Saxena said.

"Was that unusual?" I asked.

"Yes, he rarely said it," he said.

"What about your wife? How was his relationship with her?"

"It was fine. They were a lot closer before. My wife felt a little insecure about Karan being closer to me. He used to rely a lot on his mother before, because of this she worried a lot about him. After he became closer to me, I think she was jealous of our bond. I feel it's quite natural for a mother to feel this way," he said and went quiet and then continued, "but yes, they were fine."

"Oh okay," said Mr. Das.

"Please tell us about the relationship between the boys?" asked Mr. Das.

"It has been fine, like regular siblings," he said and started sobbing.

"We understand sir, but you need to help us help you," I said.

"Karan was an autistic child. He had mild autism and we tried to ensure he had a normal childhood. He was the answer to our prayers. He was everything we wanted," he said stammering.

"Right, we understand. Can you elaborate on how Sachin's relationship with Karan was?" I asked.

"Sachin and Karan were good. Sachin loved his brother. He always has. He cared for him and they always hung out together. It used to bother him that we gave more attention to Karan, but he understood. He has been a good kid. I cannot imagine how he will bear this," he said.

"Yeah, since Karan was close to you and he came to you with all his problems, did he in his recent days talk anything about his personal life? Has he shared who he's close to or who his closest friends were?" asked Mr. Das.

"He was the most close to his brother. He often shared about his day and how things were with them. But I don't know of anything or anyone else. He used to mention his friend Sarthak sometimes. Sarthak and Sachin were great friends too," he said.

"Do you doubt anyone, sir?" I asked.

"I don't know who'd want my son dead. I am clueless," he said, wiping his tears with his handkerchief.

"Thank you for your time, Mr. Saxena. We'll call you in for another round soon," I said.

After escorting him and his lawyer out, I sat next to Mr. Das, who looked deep in thought.

"This family seems difficult to crack. We can't just send out warrants because they are well-connected. Although it has been an interesting day, let's sit back later to discuss," said Mr. Das.

"Yes," I replied.

"Your phone was constantly buzzing throughout the investigation. Is everything good?" asked Mr. Das.

"It was Riya," I said.

"Oh? Well, I am sure you have a lot to discuss with her. She has been crucial to the case," he said.

"Yup, she has," I replied. I knew I wasn't seeing the crucial evidence clearly, even though it was right there in front of me.

"What? What are you thinking about?" he asked.

"Nothing, just tired. Do you think we should call for Sachin again?" I asked.

"I think we should, because there are discrepancies," he said and continued, "did we get the CCTV footage from the café and all the phone recordings?" he asked.

"Yes, CCTV from other cafes is there but the cameras were not functioning properly at Elysian! We will receive clearance to access the recordings and WhatsApp messages later this evening," I said.

"Okay great, Mr. Mehta will be assisting us with this. Please inform him once we have it all," he said.

"Yes absolutely, I am on it," I replied.

We concluded our investigation for the day. I decided to meet Riya.

Chapter 8
Riya

"Hi Babe, it feels like ages, How are you?" I asked Manav who looked terribly exhausted.

"I am fine, let's get some coffee?" he asked. He had been here for a while but I guessed he required some air.

"Yes, sure! Elysian?" I asked.

"Will that be okay with you?" he asked.

"Yes, of course, I mean I like the place. It's difficult considering I used to see Karan almost daily there, but I went there yesterday. It feels fine," I said.

"Okay then, let's go," he said. He felt a bit distant and lost.

"Is everything okay?" I asked.

"No, not really. I am just troubled with Karan's murder. I feel the entire family is messed up," he replied.

"What do you mean?" I asked, astonished but thankful that he finally decided to share things with me.

"I mean, people who are involved in the case have given me accounts of them. The investigation is not drawing any conclusions now. There were some discrepancies, but they are yet to be backed by evidence," he said.

"I am sure a family member is involved. I've read a couple of books, and it's often always the family. The parents seem cold people anyway," I said.

"Yes? Why do you say that?" he asked.

"Didn't I tell you? I happened to see them around my house one day. They were not very polite," I said.

"Hmm, okay. Let's see. I hope the murder weapon will help us now," he said.

"Yes, the knife will lead you to the killer," I said.

"Yes," he said and looked straight into my eyes.

"What happened?" I said.

"You know I love you?" he said, brushing my hair away and planting a kiss on my forehead.

"I love you too," I said and side hugged him.

"Thank you for helping me throughout, even though I have been quite busy the past few days. It's been rough," he said

"I know, I understand. You don't have to apologize to me. I am here to help you. Nobody has given me the time and attention you gave," I replied.

"Yeah, I am glad too. Let's head to the coffee house. We don't want to finish our entire conversation here," he said, smiling.

"Oh yes, let's," I said.

Tina greeted us as we entered the café. "Oh! Hi, Riya," said Tina. The murder had turned Elysian into the talk of the town, and the media had picked up on it. Such incidents are difficult to keep under wraps, regardless of how high-profile they are. People knew Karan was last seen at the Elysian, but the CCTV footage was missing due to malfunctioning cameras. It's easy to overlook the need for everything to be fully operational until something as serious as a murder happens.

"Hi, Tina! How have you been?" I asked.

"I am okay. How are you?" she replied.

"Same, Tina," I said.

"Americano right?" I asked Manav and he nodded.

"Can I please get an americano and a latte?" I asked.

"Yes, of course, I'll get it to your table," Tina replied and gestured for Harry to place the order I had requested. I noticed that this time, Tina's usual smile was missing.

Manav chose the table Karan and Sachin often took.

"Why this?" I asked, as I kept my bag and pulled out the chair to sit.

"Just," he said.

"Okay," I said and sat. It felt eerie to sit where they used to sit.

"What else can I help you with, Manav?" I asked Manav, trying to shift the attention to the case.

"Nothing, I cannot believe we haven't found any clue yet. How can a family be so messed up? It's astonishing how well-known they are in the circle, yet there's so much hidden behind their seemingly innocent faces," he said. "Who's to say Sachin is not behind all this?"

"I mean we can also assume that it is Sarthak or Mr. Saxena. But that doesn't mean that Mrs. Saxena might be innocent," I said.

Manav stared at me and said, "You should join the team. Give us your input!"

"You're joking, right?" I asked although he seemed pretty serious about it.

"No, I mean, you can come down to the interrogation office and question suspects," he said.

"No way!" I exclaimed.

"Please don't be intimidated. You can help us solve this matter at the earliest. You have observed so much here," Manav said firmly.

Just then Tina came with our coffee. She seemed to be nodding at Manav.

"I'm sorry for eavesdropping, I was clearing the table next to you. But I mean Riya, you are a regular here. I am sure you will be able to help," she said.

I was surprised. I never imagined Tina and Manav agreeing to something.

"Did you talk often to Karan?" I asked, holding the coffee from her and passing the Americano to Manav.

"Not really, he was one of our regulars. He appeared kind. It was pleasant to have him around," she said.

"Tina, the police might require you to go to the station and give your statement. I will pass on the information to the department. They were going to call you anyway, considering Karan used to come here often. I am sure you might give us an overview of things too," said Manav.

"Oh, sure. I want to help in any way I can," she said. "I am extremely sorry about the CCTV. My manager has already given me an earful on that. I know I should have informed him that it wasn't working, but I didn't think it was important. It was an honest mistake." She started sobbing, clearly unable to control her emotions.

"Hey, I am sorry. I did not mean to make this uncomfortable for you," said Manav and got up to give her a side hug. He handed over a tissue to her so she could wipe off her tears.

"Thank you," she said.

"I can't imagine how much this might have affected you," I said.

"Yes," she said and left.

I looked at Manav pointedly. He caught my eye and rolled his eyes.

"Please, I didn't mean to make it uncomfortable. It's just part of the process," he said.

"Fine, please let me know if you want my help," I said. "I am just not comfortable with going to the station and talking to strangers."

"Okay, calm down. I know it can be nerve-wracking. Whatever I have heard has been very stressful, to say the least," he said, placing his hand.

"Yes, I can do that," I said, as I sipped my Latte and continued, "What else do you want to know?"

"Alright, I'll meet you tomorrow and keep you in the loop," he said.

"Okay, whatever you say," I replied.

I noticed Tina deep in conversation with Harry. From what I had observed, neither Tina nor Harry had ever interacted with Karan and Sachin in a way that suggested any real closeness. It puzzled me why Tina, a coffee house employee, would be so willing to give a statement and take such a risk, especially when the CCTV footage clearly implicated her. Was there more to the story? Could Tina be a potential suspect as well? May be, I was overthinking and over-indulging myself. SO, let that thought pass for a while.

"By the way, Manav, I have never seen Tina being close to either Sachin or Karan. Why would she willingly testify for someone she has no relation to? And that too when she messed up. Don't you think there is something suspicious here?" I asked.

"Oh, well. I think she is just trying to be helpful," he said.

"I am just saying. Anyone could be a suspect. Anyone could have a motive," I said.

"It feels like you are pursuing the wrong profession. Join the forces," he teased.

"Do you want me to walk you home? My car's anyway parked here," he asked.

"No, please carry on. I'll finish my coffee and then head home," I said.

"Okay," he replied and got up to give me a side hug. I reciprocated.

Chapter 9
It's insane!

I woke up from my bed and turned on the TV. It was finally on the news! I immediately texted Manav, "*It's all on the news.*"

"*We know! It's a mess, call you in some time.*"

"*Oh okay, call me soon. Have you guys found the murderer? Is that what it means?*" I texted back but there was no reply from Manav.

I started shuffling through the channels to see what was being covered.

"MURDER WEAPON FOUND!!!" said one of the headlines at Sutra News.

"WHO KNEW THE KILLER WOULD BE IN HERE?" said Fast News Channel.

Killer in here? What did they mean? Had the killer been found? Or was it a metaphor? I couldn't wait for Manav to reach out to me and tell me what exactly he knew and if he could tell me. Did they mean they found the knife which was used to murder Karan or was it anything else?

"*I'll meet you soon, have to be around to sort the media mess,*" I got a text back from Manav.

So it was clear that the case was leading to something interesting. They tried so hard to keep it away from the media, but the fact that everyone now knew would make it even more important for the authorities to quickly find the murderer. I watched the news channel carefully to see if there was any progress, however, there was nothing about the killer yet.

"*Ok, waiting to see you babe,*" I texted Manav back.

"*Sure,*" he replied.

It seemed more prudent to head to the café rather than stay here, letting my anxiety build. So I headed for a hot shower to calm myself. I made myself some eggs and decided to have my coffee at Elysian. As I was packing my laptop bag, I heard my doorbell ring.

"*Who could it be?*" I murmured. I kept the bag on the bed and went to the hallway to open the door. As I unlocked the door, I saw three men standing outside my gate.

"Ma'am, are you Riya?" they asked.

"Yes, what is this about?" I asked.

"Ma'am you have to come back with us to the station in regards to the Karan Saxena murder case," said one of the men in blue. He was tall and well suited, with sharp green eyes.

"Police Station? Me? Why? Why am I called to the station like this? I didn't even know the guy," I said, bombarding them with a series of questions.

"There's nothing to worry about. We are questioning everyone who was at the café and was a regular," said another man, a tall guy with a thick moustache and spectacles on his eyes.

"Oh okay, sure but give me a moment," I said.

I immediately texted Manav, "*Hey the police are here. They're asking me to come to the police station.*"

"*Where are you, Manav?*"

"*Manav, I told you I do not want to go to the station. I can tell you everything I know. Where are you????*"

As I pretended to gather my things and get ready, I kept texting Manav.

"Miss, we are waiting," said the gentleman.

"Yeah, sure," I said and finally met them at the door. I locked the house and we headed to the station.

My heart raced as I tried to steady my nerves. New places always made me anxious, and the fact that this new place was a police station only heightened my unease. As we arrived, I saw a throng of media personnel gathered behind barriers, eagerly waiting for their next big story. We hurried inside, hoping to avoid any confrontation with the reporters. Despite our rush, I could still hear the desperate cries of, "Sir! Sir! Please listen, Sir!"

"Please wait here and you'll be called in for the interrogation", said the tall gentleman with a moustache.

"Sure," I replied. I couldn't help but scan the room, my left foot tapping on the ground incessantly. I got up to get myself some water as my throat dried up.

"Ma'am, please go there," said one of the men, gesturing to a room with a shabby-looking door. I slowly opened the door and went inside.

I couldn't believe my eyes and blurted, "Manav?" My whole world collapsed as I saw him inside. There was a pain I never experienced before. Manav managed to make me feel that love and the pain, both. My body was shaking and eyes were watering as I kept looking at Manav with utter shock and disbelief.

"Hi Riya. Please have a seat," he said.

"What? Manav, what are you doing here?" I asked, with sheer difficulty in speaking.

"Ma'am, please keep the conversations about the questions we ask about the case," said another man, who introduced himself as Mr. Das.

I was flabbergasted. How could Manav have kept this from me? After all this time, he had concealed from me that he was the interrogator. I was a fool. I loved him and I was betrayed, yet again. I should have known better.

"Manav, what is happening?" I asked, completely ignoring the question Mr. Das posed.

"Riya, we are interrogating everyone who was at the café the day Karan went missing. You were one of them," said Manav.

At that moment, my heart pounded so loudly, I was certain others could hear it.

"Okay, go ahead," I said, trying to steady my nerves and prepare myself for their questions.

"Where were you on the day Karan went missing?" Manav asked.

He already knew the answer but I needed to answer for the records. I struggled to meet his gaze as I said, "Well, I was at café, working on my PhD. I had just reached the analysis part of my review…"

I cut off mid-sentence when Mr. Das raised his right hand to stop me. "You don't need to provide details, Miss. You've already stated that you were at the café working on your PhD," Mr. Das said.

"What was Karan doing then?" Manav asked.

"Well, I wasn't specifically watching Karan, but he was there with his brother Sachin. They were having coffee, I suppose," I answered, taken aback by the question.

"How long ago did you move to Delhi, Riya?" Mr. Das asked.

"About 4-5 months ago, I think," I replied.

"And how do you like it?" he asked.

"It's good. I have settled in now," I said.

"And how long have you known Karan and Sachin?" he pressed.

"I think about 3 months. I have been a regular at the coffee house, and they have too," I replied.

"So, you understand how significant your involvement is in this case," he said.

"But I've already told Manav everything I know," I replied.

"I understand, but I need to hear it in a formal interrogation to have it on record. We need everything to be documented," he said.

"Oh, okay. I can repeat everything; I have no problem with that," I said.

"That's good. So Riya, why didn't you ever befriend the brothers?" Mr. Das asked.

"Well, I have always been an introvert. I find it hard to make friends and go to new places. I only knew them because I was a regular at the café. I'm just another face there," I replied.

"Interesting. How did you find the courage to move to a new city with no friends?" he asked.

Manav had been silently taking notes and listening to the conversation. I was still in disbelief that he had kept so much from me.

"My supervisor, Mr. Roy, thought it would be beneficial for me to be in Delhi for meetings. I felt it was a chance for change from Dehradun and might do me good," I explained.

"So, there was no other reason for your move?" he asked.

"None," I said calmly.

"Riya, where are your parents?" Manav asked.

I was taken aback by the question and shocked that he was bringing my family into this. I felt betrayed.

"They are in Dehradun," I answered tersely.

"What kind of relationship do you have with them?" he asked.

"Why are you asking about my parents? I didn't kill Karan. This conversation should end now?" I shouted.

"Calm down," said Mr. Das.

I was furious at the direction that the investigation had taken. I did not want to shout. I was just overwhelmed with anger and betrayal.

"Dad," said Manav, "please pass me the papers," gesturing towards a stack.

I stared at Manav in shock. Was Mr. Das Manav's father? Had Manav been in this profession all along?

"Riya, please tell us about your relationship with your parents," Manav asked again.

"It's been troubled. We never really bonded. They never understood me, and we were always at odds," I replied.

"Where were you on the date Karan went missing?" he asked.

"Huh? Umm, I was at the café and then went home," I replied.

"Did your parents have any issues with you moving to Delhi?" he asked.

"Yes, they did, but I have always done my own thing," I said.

"Are you sure you were home that day?" he asked again.

I paused, breathing heavily. I was still in shock over Manav's presence.

"Actually, no. I went to the university to meet my professor," I admitted. "And I met you that day, Manav."

"Yes, you did," he said. "So why were you so interested in Sachin and Karan's conversations?"

"I am just a curious person," I said.

"Curious enough to overhear?" he asked.

"What are you even doing? Just find out who used that fucking knife on Karan. Stop wasting my time," I said.

"How did you know it was a knife?" he asked.

"Huh?" I said.

Silence fell over the room.

"You told me Karan was killed with a knife," I replied, trembling.

"I didn't say a word about the weapon. How did you know it was a knife?" Manav asked.

"Listen, you should catch Sachin before he disappears," I said.

"Riya, it's time you tell us why you are in Delhi and why did you murdered Karan?" Manav said.

"Better yet, why don't we tell you," Mr. Das said.

Chapter 10

The Girl in the Coffee House

It was dark, late and I was in the room, cornered.

"Riya, you didn't move to Delhi solely for your PhD. You're adopted, aren't you?" Manav asked.

"I just have a difficult relationship with my parents," I said.

"You have a troubled relationship with them, so you killed Karan out of jealousy," he said.

"I did not murder Karan!" I shouted. "Do you understand?"

"Shut up," Mr. Das ordered, raising his voice.

"Tell us why you did it?" he asked.

"I didn't," I repeated.

"Crazy woman," Manav muttered.

"Shut up! I did not murder Karan," I insisted.

"But how did you kill him, Riya? The day Karan went missing, you went to the university. What happened in between?" Manav asked. "Your hands were dirty. Did you think you were clever, planting a knife?"

"What did you gain from this?" Mr. Das asked.

"Are you some innocent bird trying to fool everyone while you fly around freely?" Manav taunted.

"Or did you think you could just roam around after committing murder?" Mr. Das added.

They continued with their barrage of questions and taunts. I was sweating, tears of anger streaming down my face.

"Yes! Yes, I killed him! That fucker had everything I was denied. Those Saxenas gave me up because of my autism. I found out Karan and Sachin were my brothers, and Karan was autistic too. Why did he get everything I didn't? I ended up in an adoption house, and then with terrible people. What the world doesn't give you, you snatch it away from the world! He deserved it," I said, gasping for breath.

"What exactly happened on the day Karan disappeared?" Mr. Das asked.

"I followed Karan to the jungle area behind the Hauz Khas Village. We argued fiercely. By then, I knew that he was my brother. I couldn't stand how fake he was. He had to be removed for me to be happy. So I killed him," I said.

"How?" Mr. Das asked. "The knife was just a distraction, which you failed at," asked Mr. Das.

"I used a tree branch and put it right through his neck. I kept stabbing him with the branch until I was sure he was dead. I planted the knife to mislead you. I knew you fools would take it as the murder weapon," I said with fury in my eyes.

"I knew it, when you met me at university with a wound on your hand. Your continuous questioning on the murder, your relentless attempts at driving me into Sachin's direction, you lurking at the murder scene and lying to me. I knew I had to dig deeper. But what did you get out of this Riya?" asked Manav.

"I got my peace. He did not deserve a future – a future that was rightfully mine. He did not deserve the trips, the love, the warmth. It was all mine but he had it. Why?" I replied.

"Step-brothers," said Mr. Das and Manav smiled.

"What?" I asked.

"The apple doesn't fall too far from the tree," said Manav. "Your mother died right after giving birth to you. It was initially reported as a natural death, but further investigation revealed the truth. Your father and your step-mother, who is your mother's sister, were in love. Your father killed your mother, after discovering your autism and put you up for adoption. And now, here you are, just like him," Manav said.

I was furious, enraged, I wanted to kill my father too.

"I have no remorse for what I did. I don't care what happens now. All I know is Karan deserved this. Life has been unfair to me and I know you will not understand this," I said.

"And you will get what's coming for you. After all, you were just a girl in the coffee house who became entangled with those boys," said Manav.